"Dusty!" The girl screamed in warning.

Spinning round, Dusty saw the two men reaching hipwards in a manner which suggested only one thing. His hands crossed in a sight-defying flicker, the matched guns sliding clear of leather, blued barrels glinting dully as they lined.

"Just try it!"

The men sat still for both knew they'd called the play wrong. Here was no dressed-up kid trying to appear tough. This was the real thing, one of the fast guns and more deadly dangerous than any they'd ever seen.

Dusty walked forward and looked down at the two scared gunmen. "All right, on your feet, both of you."

The men scrambled up fast. One of them licked his lips and said, "We was only funning, mister."

"Why sure," Dusty drawled and holstered his guns. "I like a good laugh." His right fist smashed into the jaw of one man and, in the same move, lashed the fist backhanded into the other's face.

THE RIO HONDO
KID

CORGI BOOKS
A DIVISION OF TRANSWORLD PUBLISHERS LTD

THE RIO HONDO KID
A CORGI BOOK 552 07897 2

Originally published in Great Britain
by Brown Watson Ltd.

PRINTING HISTORY
Corgi edition published 1968
Corgi edition reprinted 1969
Corgi edition reprinted 1972
Corgi edition reprinted 1976

This book is set in 9-10 pt. Times

Corgi Books are published by Transworld Publishers Ltd.,
Century House, 61–63 Uxbridge Road,
Ealing, London, W.5.
Made and printed in Great Britain by
Hunt Barnard Printing Ltd., Aylesbury, Bucks.

The rider came into view, halting his seventeen hand, white stallion and looked down at the small, stone-built house. His eyes took in the white picket fence which surrounded the property, the truck and flower gardens and the small area where the Mahons' pair of milk cows grazed. He glanced next at the well by the side of the house, then once more at the girl. Kneeing his horse forward he allowed it to walk down the slope.

Once more Lindy lowered the hoe, straightening her back and looking at the approaching man with interest. There was a hint of panic in her eyes as she saw the way he sat his horse. He rode with the easy grace of a cowhand and in the Gunn River Valley country cowhands were no longer the most welcome people for a nester. The girl studied the rider closely deciding she had never seen him around the town of Escopeta or in the Valley.

He was tall. That was obvious even as he sat the huge white horse. She put his height at around the six foot mark and there was a lean, whipcord strength about him: wild, alien, almost Indian. It showed in the easy grace of his riding but more so in the cautious way his eyes examined the surrounding country. On his head was a low-crowned, wide-brimmed black Stetson hat. His hair, from what Lindy could see of it, was also black: so black it almost looked blue. His face was handsome, dark and very young-looking, a strangely innocent face. Around his throat, tight rolled and knotted was a black silk bandana, the ends hanging over his black shirt. All his clothing, including the gunbelt, was black: relieved only by the walnut grips of the old Colt Dragoon revolver holstered butt forward at his right side and the ivory hilt of the bowie knife sheathed at his left.

Lindy's attention never left the man. She tried to act as if he was not there or as if she did not care if he was there or not, but failed. The horse was a beauty, one of the finest she had ever seen: big but far from slow or clumsy, giving the impression of being as light on its feet as a mountain goat and meaner than two starving silvertip grizzlies. The saddle, as might be expected of a man who dressed in such a manner, was a good Texas rig, low horned and double girthed. A long Manila rope was coiled and strapped to the saddlehorn; the rider's bedroll fastened to the saddle's cantle and from under his left leg rose tthe butt of a Winchester rifle in a leather

6

boot. Even at that distance the girl could see it was no ordinary Winchester, the woodwork was black, not brown, and shone in the light of the sun.

She felt disturbed by the sight of the young-looking man who was riding towards her. There was something latent, deadly and dangerous about him despite his youthful appearance. It was not the gun, nearly every man in the West wore at least one gun, particularly when riding alone and near an Indian reservation and the White Mountain Apache reservation was less than ten miles from the Gunn River. No, she decided, it was something deeper than that, a vague instinct she could not account for.

Yet for all of that there was nothing menacing or alarming in the young cowhand's attitude as he brought his horse to a halt outside the fence. He removed his hat as the girl came towards him, his voice, as he greeted her, a pleasant southern drawl.

"Howdy, ma'am. I rode a considerable piece since sunup. Take it kind if I could water my hoss."

Lindy looked at him. The Gunn River was just beyond the next rim, not more than half a mile away. He must be a stranger or he would know that. But the place had a well in the grounds and company would be welcome. Then she saw his eyes. They were a curious red-hazel colour, hard eyes, old eyes, eyes which did not go with such an innocent and young-looking face. Lindy guessed he was a Texan. A man did not dress, ride, or talk like that unless he was a son of the Lone Star State and real proud of it. She made her decision. Cowhand he was, hard, tough fighting man he might be, but he was a traveller and as such could expect certain hospitality.

"Of course," she said, indicating the well. "Come in and draw some water."

The young man swung down from his horse at the invitation; it was the way of the land never to dismount unless invited to do so. Opening the gate, he entered with the big white horse on his heels like a well-trained hound-dog. The Texan looked at the girl, liking what he saw.

Lindy was suddenly conscious of his gaze and wished she was not wearing an old, torn, gingham dress. She was a plump though shapely girl with mousy brown hair. Her face was pretty and friendly, the sort of face which was meant to have a smile on it. Her blue eyes were alight with

7

merriment and showed an inner joy mingled with a love of the world in general. She saw how handsome this young man was and wished she was wearing her best dress and shoes instead of being barefoot and clad in a tight, torn old frock.

Then she smiled; the young stranger did not look more than sixteen years old; too young for a mature woman of eighteen.

"Thanks, ma'am," he said, making for the well. "Sure is hot today."

"It's always hot in New Mexico," she pointed out.

"So they tell me, ma'am," he drawled, although he sounded as if he did not believe anything he was told. "It's hotter than this, even in the middle of winter, back home to Texas."

Lindy smiled, thinking how like a Texas man that was. They always held that Texas was bigger, wider, hotter, colder than any other place in the world. She walked alongside him to the well, noticing the almost Indian silence as he put his feet down on the ground. She got the impression he could walk over sun-dried sticks without making a sound.

At the well the young man let down the bucket and drew up water for his big horse. Her attention was drawn to the white again, for Lindy was Western enough to know a real fine horse when she saw one. Her eyes were glowing with admiration and she reached out to pat the sleek white neck. Instantly the young man's hand shot out, catching her wrist and holding it. She felt a momentary panic and tried to jerk free.

"Don't try and touch him, ma'am," said the Texan, his voice still friendly, but with an urgent note of warning. He released her wrist and went on, "Sorry if I scared you, but this ole Nigger hoss of mine don't take to folks touching him . . . not even me."

With this he reached out a hand to pat the horse's neck. The white snapped at him, teeth clicking scant inches from his arm as he avoided the bite. The Texan laughed, slapping the muzzle, then allowing the horse to drink from the bucket. Lindy watched the byplay between man and horse, then asked:

"Would he really bite me?"

"Sure would, ma'am. See, ole Nigger's part catch-dawg, part-cougar, with just enough hoss throwed in to let a man ride him sometimes."

8

The house door opened and Mrs. Mahon came out, squinting against the light as she looked at the cowhand. She felt a momentary panic at seeing the young man talking with her daughter. Then she saw he was a stranger, a drifter passing through. To a Western woman this was a heavensent opportunity to hear some fresh talk and news of the outside world.

"Who is it, Lindy?" she called.

"A stranger just passing through, mama," answered Lindy. "He stopped to water his horse and get a drink for himself."

Mrs. Mahon walked towards them and the young man turned to greet her with the same politeness he had showed Lindy. He did not need to be told who she was, there was enough family likeness between the girl and her mother to make it unnecessary. The woman was looking at him. She thought at first he was just a youngster travelling from one job to another. Now she could tell he was a hard, tough man full grown and older than he first appeared. He might look sixteen, but if that was his true age they had been sixteen hard packed, dangerous years.

"You look hungry, young man," she said, after looking him over. "Come in and take something with us."

"Why thank you, ma'am. A man gets tired of his own fixings."

"Turn your horse to graze behind the house, if you think he won't stray," Mrs. Mahon said, "then come in. Leave the hoeing, girl, and take care of our guest."

Lindy followed the young man and watched him loosen the girths of the saddle. "Why do you have two cinches?" she asked, as he allowed the horse to walk away.

"Makes it safer, only we call them girths in Texas," he explained. "Texas man ropes something, he figures to hang on to it . . . so he ties his rope to the horn. A single girth rig won't stand up to that, so we use two of 'em."

His eyes were constantly moving, looking around him. He saw the lean-to behind the house and the old buggy and plough, then made a careful scrutiny of the country.

Satisfied all was well, he followed the girl around the side of the building to the front. Lindy opened the door and entered first. He followed, stepping into the cool passage which ran the length of the house. On the left side were three doors, he guessed they led to the bedrooms. The doors on the right would lead into living room and kitchen. The whole

9

place was clean and neat, with the care and attention a woman would lavish on her home. The girl led him into the first door on the right, his guess was correct, it was the living room. Telling him to sit at the table, Lindy left, making for the kitchen to help her mother.

The young Texan sat in a straight-back chair at the table, looking around the room. There were a couple of paintings on the wall and gay curtains at the windows. The room was like the rest of the house, clean and homely, the furniture not new but good quality. Over the fireplace, on pegs, hung an old singleshot, Springfield rifle, one of the earliest models, chambered for metallic cartridges. By it was an old Union Army pistol belt; the holster's flap was cut off and a revolver butt showing. The young man studied the holster, seeing that a fast draw would be almost impossible with such a rig. The gun was unusual, a type he had rarely seen and not in recent years; a Pettingill Navy revolver, hammerless, percussion fired and long out of date. Unless the man of the house was carrying better weapons with him they would be in bad trouble if ever attacked. Anyone living near an Apache reservation needed better weapons than an old, singleshot rifle and a percussion-fired revolver of such light calibre. His own revolver was percussion fired, but it was a Colt Dragoon, .44 in calibre and effective. Besides that, he owned a Winchester repeating rifle.

Lindy and her mother came into the room, the girl carrying a loaded tray. She set it down on the table and passed the Texan a plate of bacon and eggs and a steaming cup of coffee. Handing the second cup to her mother she took the third herself and sat down. There was no talking, the Texan ate with the healthy appetite of a young man who had not bothered to cook himself a meal since noon the previous day. He finished the meal, then took up the coffee-cup and smiled at the two women.

"Thanks for the meal, ma'am. My cooking's not what it used to be—fact being, it never was."

Mrs. Mahon laughed, then seeing the bulge of a tobacco sack in the Texan's vest pocket gave him permission to smoke. He took out the tobacco, spread a paper and rolled a cigarette, then carried on with the conversation.

"Nice place you've got here, ma'am."

"It is. But you look like a big ranch man, yourself."

10

"Man'd say you were right, ma'am," agreed the Texan, pride in his voice. "The biggest of them all. I ride for the OD Connected, in the Rio Hondo country of Texas. The name's Loncey Dalton Ysabel."

It was a name which meant nothing to Lindy or her mother, but in Texas or among the cowhands in New Mexico, it would have meant plenty.

Loncey Dalton Ysabel, the Ysabel Kid, was well enough known. He rode for the OD Connected ranch, a member of the elite of the ranch, Ole Devil Hardin's floating outfit. More, he was the particular friend and sidekick of the segundo of the ranch, the Rio Hondo gun wizard, Dusty Fog. The Ysabel Kid, son of a wild Irish-Kentuckian father and a French Creole-Comanche mother. From his father he inherited a love of fighting and the rifle skill of a legendary back-woodsman of old. From his mother came a skill with horses; the inborn skill of the finest tribe of horse-Indians, and the love of cold steel as a fighting weapon, a love which led him to carry that James Black bowie knife wherever he went. He was fair with his old Second Model Dragoon, fair when it meant to be able to draw and shoot in a second—and hit his man at the the end of that time. To these talents was added an ability to read sign and follow tracks where a buck Apache might falter; also a fluent knowledge of Spanish and six Indian tongues. Wherever cowhands met and talked, the Ysabel Kid was known as a fighting man, a real good friend and a real bad enemy.

But neither of the women knew this. They noticed how he spoke with pride about his ranch, but this was not unusual. Most cowhands were proud of their brand. To the women the Ysabel Kid was still the same young, friendly, yet somehow dangerous, cowhand they brought in for a meal.

Disappointment tinged Lindy's voice as she looked at the Kid. "You're a big ranch man, then?"

"Like I said, the biggest of them all," the Kid replied amiably. "You sound like you don't cotton to big ranch men. Now me, I don't care. Big or small it don't make no never mind to me."

"It does in Gunn River County," Mrs. Mahon replied, trying to keep the bitterness out of her voice. "Or, it does to the big ranch men."

There was nothing but polite interest in the Kid's voice as

11

he drawled, "You sound like you're having troubles, ma'am."

The answer came fast, too fast. "We've no trouble."

"No, ma'am?" the Kid answered, his voice showing nothing that he felt.

"All right, we are having trouble with the big ranchers."

"Not with the Lazy S, mama," Lindy corrected. "Mary Simmonds and her father are trying to find out who's making all the trouble."

Mrs. Mahon nodded, then a sudden suspicion came to her and she looked at the Kid. "Are you going to work around here?"

"No, ma'am. I helped take a herd to ole Texas John Slaughter's place over to Arizona, now I'm heading home again. I couldn't agree with my two pards which'd be the best way for us to go, so we split up for a spell. Mark and Dusty went along to see some of Mark's kin and I cut through Azul Rio county. We're meeting up again in Escopeta today, unless they're late, which same they allus are."

That was true enough as far as it went. The Ysabel Kid's true purpose in going to Azul Rio county was to carry on a casual flirtation with a certain pretty señorita. Unfortunately, Juanita Estradre's father was hospitable and the Kid stayed longer than he intended. Now he was heading to meet his friends two days later than promised. They would be waiting for him in Escopeta, ready to wax sarcastic about people who came late.

"Then you won't be working hereabouts?" Mrs. Mahon asked, sounding relieved. He would make a bad enemy and she was pleased to hear he would not be riding for any of the five big ranches which shared Gunn River County with the nesters.

"Not me, ma'am. This's a no-good section. I wouldn't work here if they was to pay me what I'm worth."

"Could you live on that little?" Lindy asked, knowing he would not take any offence at her words.

"Huh! New Mexico," snorted the Kid.

"You can always tell a Texan," Lindy scoffed.

"Why sure. But you can't tell us much," the Kid replied. He turned back to Mrs. Mahon and went on. "Are the big ranch boys causing fuss with you folks?"

"Not with us directly, but with the other farmers in the valley."

"It been happening long?"

"Over the last three months. We all got on well at first, have done for a few years. Then some of the farmers started to find cattle driven over their growing crops, fences ripped down. There were even a couple of barns went up in flames."

"That's all on your side, ma'am," the Kid remarked, his face showing nothing of what he felt. "How about the ranchers?"

"*They* say they've been losing cattle, finding stock butchered and waterholes either fenced off, or spoiled. I don't know how true it is. All I know is every farm except ours has been in some kind of trouble."

"With the big ranchers, way you see it. Why'd you reckon they want you out of the valley?"

"I don't know," Mrs. Mahon replied, wondering if this young man was getting interested in their problems. "There's more than enough water and land for all of us. We all used to get along well enough until about three months ago. We bought beef or old horses from the ranchers, they bought hay and truck from us, then the trouble began. Of course it might be Apaches causing the trouble."

The Ysabel Kid shook his head. He knew Apaches far better than they.

"Apaches might take cattle. Fact being, the way they get fed on the reservations they often have to. But Indians wouldn't waste time in butchering stock. They take beef on the hoof and save having to tote it. Besides, Apaches wouldn't fence waterholes and they wouldn't stop at just burning barns. They'd either keep at peace with the white-eyes, or be out wearing paint."

That was one expression neither woman needed explaining. They knew an Apache put on his paint before going to war. Lindy was about to remark on this when she saw the young man stiffen slightly. Suddenly there was a change in him, he was tense and alert.

"You expecting six—eight riders, ma'am?" he asked.

Mrs. Mahon shook her head. She strained her ears but could make out no sound. At first she thought her guest was imagining things, then faintly she heard the sound of hooves. The sound grew in volume as the riders approached the house. Her eyes met Lindy's the same thought in both minds: was this to be the start of trouble?

13

Then Mrs. Mahon looked at the Ysabel Kid, wondering if he knew more than he said about the approaching riders. If he was working with them he would not have mentioned their coming. Mrs. Mahon licked her lips worriedly, her mouth felt dry. It might prove to have been a bad mistake, inviting the young man into the house, and letting him see there was no man present.

Lindy pushed back her chair, then ran to the window. She felt sick and afraid at what she saw. Eight men sat their horses just beyond the picket fence, eight grim-faced men. The biggest of them shouted as she looked out.

"Mahon! Mahon. Come out of there, we want to talk to you!"

Mrs. Mahon was pale as she came to her feet. She glanced at the young Texas man but he sat back, not moving or showing any interest. Without a word Mrs. Mahon turned and walked from the room, along the passage and opened the front door. The eight riders tensed in their saddles as the door opened, then relaxed when they saw it was a woman coming out. Mrs. Mahon looked the men over, they wore cowhand's clothes, but she could not say which ranch they were from.

"My husband isn't here!" said Mrs. Mahon, trying to hide her fear.

The biggest of the men laughed harshly. "Tod, Sam, go in there and drag him out!"

Two of the men swung from their saddles, walking to the gate, kicked open the gate and stepped into the ground. Mrs. Mahon opened her mouth to say something, then a hand gripped her arm and she was drawn into the house. She saw the Ysabel Kid move by her, stepping into the garden to one side of the door. In that brief instant she caught a glimpse of his face and wondered how she had ever thought of him as young and innocent.

"That's far enough!" said the Ysabel Kid, not raising his voice. The soft words brought the two men to a halt.

All eyes were on him now, reading him for what he was. It took more than an innocent face to fool men like these. They could read the signs and knew this was no boy but a man grown in the land, a man the peer of any of them.

The big man who had done all the talking studied the Kid,

14

then called. "Them's lousy sod-busters you're siding, boy. Shy out of it."

"The lady's telling you true. Her man isn't here."

The Ysabel Kid's right hand hung negligently at his side, palm turned out near the walnut grips of his old gun. He watched the men all the time, no move overlooked.

"You ain't backing nesters, are you?" the big man asked.

"Like the lady said," growled the Kid, Comanche mean, "her man isn't home—now I'm telling you."

Putting it that way the Ysabel Kid gave the men no choice: they either took his word or called him a liar. It was as easy as that. The men on foot were worried, they were close in and would bear the brunt of any hostilities. One of them looked over his shoulder at the men behind.

"What about it, Lloyd?"

The big man's hand dropped to his side before he replied. It was a casual move and would have gone unnoticed by a less suspicious man than the Ysabel Kid.

"Go get Mahon out of there!"

The Kid's right hand twisted, lifting the old Dragoon clear of leather in a smooth cavalry draw. His left hand was chopping to knock back the hammer as he dropped to the ground. The old Colt boomed out just as he hit the hard-packed dirt of the path.

Lloyd rocked back in the saddle, smashed against the cantle by the round lead ball powered by a full forty grain of powder. His horse reared wildly, throwing all the others into confusion and hindering the riders. The men shot wildly at the smoke-wrapped figure in front of the house.

The Kid was on the ground, his old Dragoon booming and black powder smoke whirling eddies around him. One of the two men in the garden spun around, a hole between his eyes and the back of his head burst open. Even as he went down the second man screamed: the ball hit him on the knee, cutting the leg from under him. Another of the Kid's bullets struck a horse, felling it, the rider kicking his legs free and dropping clear.

By this time the gunmen were more or less in control of their horses and shooting back. The thick pall of powder smoke hid the Kid and made him a poor mark. But his old gun was empty and he knew he would soon be facing the music; the wind would shift the powder smoke. He whistled and heard the big white horse coming towards him. If he could get to the rifle in the saddle-boot and find shelter at the side of the house he would make the men wish they had never come.

The Kid came to his feet in a fast, lithe move, hurling himself towards the horse. He felt a blow as lead caught him and was slammed back into the wall of the house, going down before his hands could reach the butt of his rifle. Lying on the ground, red mists of agony welling through him, the Kid wondered why other bullets were not smashing into him, and what the weight on him was.

Lindy Mahon had joined her mother by the door when the Kid went out. She had watched the fight and seen the Kid take lead. Without any thought for her own safety she flew from the house and dropped, covering him with her own body. The men held their fire for they would not risk killing a woman. They dismounted, and a tall, heavy-set man, opened the gate and came into the grounds. Gun in hand he walked forward, passing the Kid's victims. The wounded one groaned out and the man stopped, looked at the girl as she crouched over the Kid's body and holstered his gun.

"He's cashed in, anyways. That boy could fight."

"Sure. And I lost me a hoss," another answered, his eyes went to the big white. "I'll take that one."

The first man looked down at the terrible wound in the victim's leg, made a wry face and asked, "What the hell was that kid using?"

"Dragoon," the other answered. "I'd as soon be hit by a buffalo gun."

"And me,' the first man replied, then turned and called. "Load Lloyd on his hoss, boys. Then come in and get these two." He looked at the other man who was going towards the Kid's big white horse. "I wouldn't touch him was I you, Sanger. Take Tod's hoss, he don't need it."

Sanger stopped, looking the big white over and seeing it was a fine animal. He disregarded the advice and stepped nearer, hand reaching out towards the white's reins. Nigger watched the man, then snorted and charged, rearing high; iron-shod hooves slashing at the air. Sanger jumped back, yelling in fright. He missed death by scant inches for the horse was a killer. One of the men leapt on his horse and rode forward, unstrapping a rope as he came. He threw and dropped a noose over the white's head. Nigger knew a rope, and knew the futility of fighting one, so stood still, snorting.

Sanger, still shaking at his narrow escape, dropped his hand to the butt of his gun. Fingers gripped his wrist, holding the gun in leather. Snarling angry curses Sanger looked into the face of the big, heavy-set man.

"What the hell, Jarman?" he said. "I'm going to kill that hoss."

"No, you aren't," Jarman answered, pushing the other man away from him. "I'm going to take it into Escopeta. Banjo'll pay well for a hoss as good as that white. Take it out there, Smith. Sanger, get a couple of hosses here and load Tod and Sam on them." With that he turned his attention to the girl again. "He dead, gal?"

Lindy's tear-stained face lifted to look at the man. "He's dead! Keep away from us and leave him alone!"

Jarman did not attempt to go near the girl. The young cowhand must be dead so there was nothing to be gained in staying. Mahon was not at home, that was for sure. The farmer was no coward and would have been outside helping the Texan fight. He looked to see that his orders were being carried out. Two men were loading the dead gunman on Lloyd's horse, fastening him behind the body of their leader. With this done they helped the groaning, barely conscious man on to another horse, after fastening a tourniquet to his leg. Then they left the garden and Jarman gave his attention to the girl.

"You nesters get out of the Gunn River Valley. Your hired gun didn't help you at all. Who was he?"

"His name was Loncey Dalton Ysabel," sobbed Lindy although the name meant nothing to her.

"Loncey Dalton Ysabel?" Jarman repeated automatically. "The Ysabel Kid?"

Lindy did not answer, her face turned to the still form beneath her. She did not see the worried frown on Jarman's face as he heard that name. Turning, he walked from the garden and mounted his horse. His men were looking to him for orders.

"Sam here's going to need a doctor," Sanger growled.

Jarman agreed but there was a big objection. The only doctor within miles was Doc Bohasker in Escopeta. He would be curious when he saw the wound; he would also put two and two together when he heard about the fight at the Mahon place.

"What we going to do, now Mahon ain't here?" the man leading Nigger went on. "The boss wanted him bad."

Jarman was thinking of this. "We can't do what the boss wants, but we can play it another way." His eyes went to the wounded man who was roped in the saddle and unconscious. "Sanger, you take Tod and Lloyd, sink them in a good deep hole in the Gunn River and make sure they don't come up. Then take Sam to the other boys. Leave him there with Simmonds, if the boys got him."

"What good'll that do?" Sanger asked. "And what you going to be doing?"

"Leave Sam there, make sure he can't talk. It'll look near on the same as the way the boss planned it. I'm going into town with Smith, take this hoss and sell it to Banjo. We'll share out what he gives us for it."

Sanger did not care for the idea but did not argue. Jarman was a good man with a gun and would not take kindly to argument. The two groups separated, going their different ways. Jarman was worried as he rode, worried and making plans. He did not intend splitting the money for the horse. The moment he was paid for the big white he was going to put many miles between Escopeta and himself. He had helped kill a member of Ole Devil Hardin's floating outfit. Every other member of that dangerous and gunhandy crew would be looking for the men who had done the shooting.

CHAPTER TWO

Where Did You Get That Horse?

ESCOPETA CITY lay in a bend of the Gunn River, a small, quiet, peaceful cattle town. The business section of town, Military Avenue, stretched straight as a die from the Gunn River saloon at the eastern end to the Banking House saloon at the west side. Along this straight, wide street lay the stores, livery-barn, jail and county offices. Beyond it the houses of the citizens were scattered and built with little conformation to lines or streets.

Frank Gunn's River Saloon was the oldest building in town. It could not compete in appearance with the more modern and garish Banking House Saloon, which might appear to be its rival for trade. This did not worry Frank Gunn, he never regarded the Banking House as a rival but rather as a useful adjunct, which syphoned off the rowdy cowhand trade. Frank Gunn's business was assured; the citizens of the town used his place, the ranchers found it a quiet haven, and the leaders of the nesters came there to get away from the noise of the Banking House. It was an ideal arrangement. The Banking House attracted the younger bloods for it offered the companionship of several pretty girls.

The Gunn River saloon offered nothing like that, nor such innovations as roulette, vingt-et-un, faro or chuck-a-luck. The only game played was poker; the play was high and the right to sit in much sought after.

The owner of the Banking House, Horace Rangoon, ran it well, insisting that his girls dressed with decorum and behaved well, both at work and away from it. His games were scrupulously honest and open to inspection at any time. Rangoon might be a dude, but he was liked in Escopeta. A small, chubby, friendly-looking man with some money behind him, he had not been long in Escopeta but already ran the saloon, a ranch in the back country and a bank. The latter was small, merely the back room of the saloon, but it was a bank for all that and he conducted much business. All in all Rangoon was liked, respected and admired, a real nice little man.

Two men rode into Escopeta in the early morning, coming by the western trail and passing the hospitable doors of the Banking House saloon. A contrasting pair in some ways, but in others they were much alike. They both wore two guns and both rode a magnificent seventeen hand stallion, the taller man on a bloodbay, the smaller afork a paint. They looked like any other drifting cowhands, yet each was a legend in his own life. Their names were Dusty Fog and Mark Counter.

The taller rider was Mark Counter, six foot three; a handsome blond giant, with great shoulders and a lean waist. His hair was curly, golden blond and his face like a Greek god of old. He sat his horse with an easy grace, a light rider despite his size. The former Beau Brummel of old Bushrod Sheldon's Confederate cavalry was now a cowcountry fashion-plate. His white, low-crowned, wide-brimmed Stetson bore a leather band with silver conchas on it. His tan shirt was costly and a good fit. His brown levis hung cowhand style, cuffs turned back and outside his high-heeled, expensive, made-to-measure boots. Around his waist was a hand-carved, buscadero gunbelt; the matched, ivory-butted Colt Cavalry Peacemakers in position to be easily reached.

But he was more than just a range-country dandy. He was known as a tophand in the cowhand trade, and his ability, in a rough-house fight, was known from the Rio Grande to Montana. His skill with the matched guns was less known, for he rode in the shadow of the Rio Hondo gunwizard, Dusty Fog.

In comparison with Mark Counter's appearance Dusty Fog faded into nothing. He was a small man, yet there was a width to his shoulders and a strength about him which went far beyond his size. His face was handsome, tanned and strong. A face which smiled easily, yet showed intelligence, command and strength of will. His hair, beneath the low-crowned Stetson hat, was a dusty blond colour. His clothing was new but he did not set it off in Mark's eye-catching way. Dusty Fog might have been a wrangler, a chore boy or a young hand just learning the cattle business. That was the impression at first sight — but not when the chips were down and the bone-handled Colt Civilian Peacemakers swept from where they lay butt forward, in the holsters of his gunbelt.

A man might wonder how such an insignificent young man came to be riding so fine a horse as the big paint. The same man would never guess that Dusty Fog was segundo of the great OD Connected ranch; that he'd been a Confederate cavalry captain at seventeen and that he was known both as town-taming lawman and as trail boss. Dusty did not look the part, but it was true. In the Civil War he rode as a captain in the Texas Light Cavalry and gained a name as being the equal of such expert raiders as John Singleton Mosby and Turner Ashby. Twice, since the War, Dusty had tamed and brought law to bad, wild, open towns.* He'd also become known as a top hand of the gunfighting fraternity, one of the élite group who owned and wore Gaylin gunbelts.

A belt meant that man was more than just one of the top guns. Old Joe Gaylin, the El Paso leatherworker, would sell his saddles or boots to any man who could meet his high prices; not so his gunbelts. He chose the men who wore his belts, chose them and made each belt with care and attention. There were not more than thirty in the West. Dusty had one, Mark Counter another. A third was owned by another member of the floating outfit who stayed at the OD Connected.

Dusty and Mark rode slowly along the street, headed for the livery barn. The few people about at that early hour gave them no more than a passing glance. At the door of the barn the two men swung down from their horses and led them into the cool of the building. The owner, Blinky Holmes, watched, studying them with eyes which knew cowhand sign and read them for what they were.

"Ole Nigger's not here, Mark," said Dusty, looking at the line of stalls. He knew the Kid would never leave his horse

---

* Told in QUIET TOWN, THE TROUBLE-BUSTERS, THE MAKING OF A LAWMAN.

21

in an open corral for Nigger took exception to strange horses.

"Never thought he would be." Mark's voice was a deep, cultured Texas drawl. "Had he been here we'd never hear the last of it. I told you we shouldn't have gone visiting with Cousin Dan. We're two days late."

Dusty did not point out that it was Mark's cousin they went to visit. "Anyways, ole Lon's not here, nor likely to be unless Miss Juanita got sense and run him off."

"Howdy gents," greeted Blinky, coming forward. His eyelids flickering in the manner which gave him his name. "Rid far?"

"Fair piece," Dusty agreed.

Mark was attending to his big horse, loosening the girths and working the saddle back and forwards to cool the blood-bay's back. He knew that, along with barbers, livery barn owners were amongst the world's great gossips, so the old timer would be the best one to ask about the Ysabel Kid.

"Have you seen anything of a Texas boy, rides a big white stallion, dresses all in black. Totes a Second Model Dragoon gun and a bowie knife. Had him a real good Winchester, unless he gave it to Miss Juanita."

"Ain't seed him," answered Blinky. He could think of only one young man who answered to that description and that gave him a possible clue to these two. "Sounds tolerable fierce, toting all that armament."

"Sure does," Mark grinned, "but don't let it fool you any. He's not."

"Any other place he could leave his hoss, friend?" inquired Dusty, taking the double-girthed saddle from his paint. "We'll leave our'n here and our gear in the office, if we can. We'll be back for it if we decide to stay on."

"Ain't but the one livery in town—ain't hardly enough trade for this one, comes to that. He might be at one of the saloons. Or there's a hotel back of here, but it don't have no stables." Blinky replied, then went on to answer Dusty's second request. "There's a burro over in the corner, hang your saddles up. Leave your bed-rolls in the office. You wanting to use the corral, or have a stall each?"

"Stalls," replied Dusty. "We'll give the hosses a treat."

Blinky eyed the two stallions with the air of a man who knew horses. "Yours or mine?" he asked.

Dusty and Mark carried their saddles to the burro, the

22

inverted V-shaped structure which ran along one side of the building. A cowhand would always use a burro if one was available. One worth his salt would never neglect his saddle; without it he was helpless for the cowhand's work was almost all done from the back of a horse. Unstrapping the bedrolls, Dusty and Mark went to the office and put the bundles in the corner out of the way.

All the time Blinky was watching them with undisguised interest. He knew cowhands, knew the pair to be top hands and guessed they were outstanding. Both Dusty and Mark realized the old man was seething with curiosity and let him seeth, not offering to introduce themselves. By the unwritten law of the West, Blinky could not ask them a direct question. A man did not ask another's name. At least not twice.

"I ain't seed either of you gents afore," said Blinky, trying tact to satisfy his curiosity.

"You sure have, friend," corrected Mark. "Afore and behind. Afore when we came in here and behind when we walked away from you. Mind you, ole Dusty here looks better from behind."

Dusty favoured Mark with a look of disgust, then turned to Blinky and lowered his voice to a confidential whisper. "Truth is, Mark and I haven't been this way before. We came to see what they did with the leavings when they finished Texas."

Blinky snorted in annoyance. He was New Mexico born and proud of it. "If Texas's so good how come the Grand Canyon's in Arizona?"

"Just goes to show the folks in Arizona don't know when to stop," Dusty answered. "If that *hombre* we were asking about comes in looking for us, tell him we came and have gone to the Gunn River for a meal."

"Who'll he ask for?"

"Likely to ask for near on anybody," replied Dusty, grinning.

Blinky showed his disgust as he studied every detail of their dress and armament. His next question bordered on the verge of polite frontier conversation. "How'll I be able to tell him your names if he does ask?"

Dusty and Mark were already walking towards the doors. They halted and looked at the old man. A mischievous smile played on Dusty's lips as he said:

"Why, ole Lon's known us for years now. He knows our names."

Before the enraged, spluttering Blinky could say another word the two young men had walked through the doors. He stopped, muttering to himself, a crafty gleam in his eyes. Turning, he went towards the stall to see what brands the horses carried. He stopped, an angry grunt coming from his lips. The two big stallions stood facing him, he could not read their brands. Curious or not, Blinky was too wise a man to enter the stalls. Any man who did, if he was a stranger to either paint or bloodbay, would not walk out again and would not be nice to carry out, either.

"Huh!" grunted Blinky, eying the horses in the same way he had looked at their masters. "Texas men and Texas hosses is all alike. Awkward, plumb awkward." He scratched his head thoughtfully. "Now who be ye? Dusty and Mark! Naw, it can't be." Turning, he ambled towards the office, then stopped as a thought struck him. "Wes Hardin's in town. Wonder if they're looking for him?"

Unaware of the speculation they had aroused, Dusty and Mark walked along the sidewalk, making for the Gunn River Saloon. They could see no sign of either the Ysabel Kid or his horse and Nigger stood out in any crowd, for there were few as big and well-shaped as the white stallion.

Being new to this section, Dusty and Mark gave the town a little attention. Escopeta was no different from many another cowtown they had seen in their travels around the country. It was pleasant enough but nothing when compared with such cowland capitals as Dodge City, Newton, Hays, Fort Worth or El Paso. The few people they saw were either nesters or cowhands.

The two Texans could feel an undercurrent of dislike and distrust between the two groups. Nesters and cowhands made a dangerous mixture and rarely came together without some kind of trouble. The dislike showed on the faces of the nesters as they passed, for Dusty and Mark were cowhands, tough gun-toting cowhands. In a town where dislike had turned to open war, such men as Dusty and Mark would fight for the ranchers.

The Gunn River Saloon was reached without incident. It was empty at this early hour of the morning, and would not have been open at all but the owner was cleaning up from the previous night's poker game. Frank Gunn put his broom by the side of the counter, mentally decided that he would change his rule of, *"Win or lose, the game closes at eight thirty in the morning,"* and went behind the bar to greet the two customers. He leaned his elbows on the bar, watching the two men. Gunn was big, almost as big and broad as Mark Counter. His shirt neck was open and stained with sweat from the all-night game. He was tired but always a good host and never turned away custom. Frank Gunn was an accomplished talker, and a better listener. He could, and liked to, talk and listen on any given subject: there were few better informed men in New Mexico Territory.

"Howdy," Mark greeted, halting at the bar. "Two beers and take something yourself."

Gunn reached under the bar, producing three bottles of beer: he made it a rule to drink the same as his customers. He opened the bottles and slid glasses along the bar to Dusty and Mark. His eyes studied them, eyes, which read the signs as well as had the old-timer at the livery barn. He could see Dusty and Mark were good with their guns and wondered if they were looking for Wes Hardin, who was at the Banking House saloon after playing in the poker game. Wes Hardin, the notorious Texas gunfighter was in Escopeta, under the thin alias of Johnson, to play poker — and avoid the Texas law.

Frank Gunn shook his head when Mark inquired after the Ysabel Kid. He noted the description given and was thoughtful. He was interested in the newcomers, more so because of certain happenings in Gunn River County.

"Do you serve food, friend?" inquired Dusty, picking up his glass.

"Sure, got me a Mex who cooks a mite. I'll tell him to throw some more food in the pan for you. What'll it be, french fried, eggs and ham?"

"We got a choice?" Mark asked.

"Not unless you want to go out, rope and butcher a steer." With that Gunn turned and yelled an order for two more meals. A blistering retort in Spanish echoed from the kitchen.

"Reckon it'll be french fried, ham and eggs, then," said Dusty, then turned to Mark. "We'll give Lon a couple more days, looks like we beat him here."

"He often late?" Gunn inquired, joining in the conversation once more.

"Sure. Only one I've seen worse is Mark here."

Mark looked shocked at this. "*Me!* Why I've never been more than three days late—she was worth it, too."

Gunn was still studying the two Texans. He knew their kind, knew them as enemy in the War, and friend in time of peace. He was not deceived by Dusty's insignificant appearance recognising his true potential.

"Just rode in, gents?" he inquired, using the recognised opener to a conversation. It left them free to give such information as was necessary. That much and no more.

"Sure," answered Mark, "just been over to Cochise County with a herd for Texas John. Stopped in at Dan Mason's on the way back. Told us to say hello to you when we got here."

"How's Dan, ain't seen him in a coon's age?"

"Nor likely to. Cousin Dan's Diana just had her third. A right smart lil shaver he is. We wound up being godfathers."

There was a pointer in the words. Dan Mason was a Texas man who owned his own spread and was kin to some well-known Texans; one family in particular, the Counters. The big blond cowhand must be one of Rance Counter's sons; he certainly showed his father's heft. The small man called him Mark. If he was Mark Counter the smaller man must be . . .

"The name's Frank Gunn, gents."

"Howdy, I'm Dusty Fog and this is Mark Counter."

The Mexican brought food on a tray, taking it to a table. Gunn came out from behind the bar and joined the two young men. They ate the meal in silence, got their smokes going and leaned back in their chairs. Gunn pulled at his cigar. He watched his two customers and wondered if their presence in town was just an accident, or if they were here for some reason. Colt Blayne, leader of the Gunn River ranchers, was a Texas man and might have written to Ole Devil Hardin for help. Gunn hoped this was correct for with Dusty Fog, Mark Counter and the Ysabel Kid in the area there was a chance of ending the trouble.

Gunn loved his county. He had been the first white settler here; the Gunn River was called after him. He had seen it turn from a wild land where Mexicans and raiding Apaches roamed to a peaceful cattle range. He had seen the nesters come and be received as friends; and now the mysterious trouble for which there was neither reason nor cause had started. Gunn knew the effect of a range-war on a peaceful country: it would ruin many of his friends.

"Nice lil town you've got here, friend," Dusty remarked, guessing at the interest he was arousing. "Much trade for two saloons?"

"Enough. We make a living. I thought I'd lose some trade when the Banking House opened. Did at first but it works out about even."

"The other place looks all right," Mark put in, "a mite flashy though!"

"It is all right. Feller as owns it sees to that. Rangoon's a real nice lil gent. Got him good sense, hires some hard boys to keep things quiet."

But neither of the Texans were listening to him. With a gunfighter's precaution they had seated themselves facing the doors of the saloon and could see anyone passing either door or windows. Their faces set in grim lines as they saw two men riding by. Gunn turned and saw the men, one of them leading a big white horse.

Dusty gripped the edge of the table hard, his knuckles white under the skin. His eyes met Mark's as he thrust back his chair. "Let's make some talk!"

They came to their feet and walked from the saloon without a word of explanation. Their full attention was on the street, on the two men who were riding towards the Banking House saloon; and on the big white stallion one of the men led. Dusty and Mark were now sure: that horse was Nigger, they were certain of it for they knew the big white as well as they knew their own mounts. The Kid was afoot, in bad trouble. There were questions to be asked and Dusty Fog meant to see the answers were forthcoming.

The few people about watched Dusty and Mark leave the saloon and step on to the gunman's sidewalk, the centre of the street. They saw the two Texans out there and with Western insight headed for cover. Trouble was in the air, between the two young Texans and the men who were swinging from their horses in front of the Banking House saloon.

Jarman was not happy about the man with him. Smith was

27

a fool; a drunken, loud-talking fool. The gunman was relieved when they swung down at the Banking House saloon. In a few minutes Banjo would have bought the big white horse and Jarman could be on his way. News of the Ysabel Kid's death would get out soon enough and he did not want to be around. There would soon be a bunch of men here who could handle all his boss's hired guns; they would be looking for the men who killed the Kid.

"Where did you get that horse?"

Jarman half turned. His face lost its colour as he looked at the two Texas men: only a friend of the Ysabel Kid would ask such a question. Standing between the horses he studied the two young men, noting the butt forward, white-handled guns and knowing who they belonged to.

Smith turned, a truculent, drunken sneer on his face. He had been hitting a bottle on the way into town, it slowed his reactions and to his whisky-dulled brain these two men were nothing but nosy cowhands.

"What's it to you?" Smith growled, teetering on his heels.

"It belongs to our pard," Mark said, in case there was a reasonable explanation of the affair. The Ysabel Kid might have been thrown and the big white found straying, although that was not likely. Nigger would never leave his master without orders.

"We bought him, didn't we, Jarman?" Smith sneered, his drunken mind full of his own prowess.

"You're a liar, mister!" Dusty spoke in a deadly voice. "Lon wouldn't sell his horse."

"That so?" Smith's voice dropped to a snarl. "You keep pushing your face in and we'll show you how we bought the white. Won't we, Jarman?"

Jarman did not reply. He was partially hidden by the two horses and stood with his left hand gripping the hitching rail. Smith was not in the class to challenge Dusty Fog and Mark Counter to a shoot-out, but he was fool enough, and drunk enough, to try it, Jarman was scared for the first time in his life, scared and thinking fast. The Texans would be concentrating on Smith, Jarman hoped. When the shooting started he would swing himself on to the sidewalk, run round the side of the saloon and hide. The Texans did not know the town and he might escape them. Then he could get a horse and clear out of the town.

"This's the last time I'll ask," said Mark Counter grimly. "Where did you get that horse?"

Smith's hand dropped to his side; Mark Counter's right hand scooped his long-barrelled Colt from the holster. The ivory-butted gun roared, kicked up and sent lead into Smith's body, knocking him from his feet. He went down, hand clawing weakly at his chest; his gun not even clear of leather.

Jarman saw the trouble, ducked under the hitching rail and lit down on the sidewalk running for the corner of the building. He heard the crash of a shot and hoped both Texans were concentrating on Smith, allowing him to get away. It was a faint hope, for Dusty Fog was not bothering with Smith at all. Even as Jarman grabbed at the hitching rail, Dusty was moving to intercept him.

With the ability to look ahead and think as the other man was thinking, Dusty acted fast. He guessed the way Jarman was going and knew full well that Mark was able to handle the other man. He leapt forward to the sidewalk. His left hand crossed his body and the Colt slid from the right side holster. As he landed, drawing back the gun's hammer, he barked out a command.

"Hold it up there!"

Jarman saw that he had made a mistake and came round, gun leaping from leather with the speed of desperation. Even though he had never worked faster, Jarman was off balance; he got off one shot and missed. Dusty's gun roared back in answer. Flame blossomed from the muzzle of his Colt, the lead ripping into Jarman's head. Dusty shot to kill. He regretted doing it but with a man as fast as Jarman there was no time to take chances.

"How's yours, Mark?" asked Dusty.

"Cashed!" Mark replied. "And we still don't know what happened to Lon."

CHAPTER THREE

A Real Nice Little Man

MEN CAME from the saloon, pushing open the batwing doors
at the sounds of shots. Dusty Fog and Mark Counter stood
side by side, guns in hand, looking for the local law but
seeing no sign of it. The men from the saloon gathered on
to the sidewalk, looking down at the two bodies.

The first two men out of the saloon were a greater contrast
than Dusty and Mark. One was a tall, slim, handsome man
wearing the dress of a frontier gambler. His grey cutaway
coat was well tailored and his frilly bosomed shirt white.
His tight-legged, white trousers were tucked neatly into
shining boots; around his waist was a black gunbelt, a brace
of matched, pearl-handled Colt Peacemakers thrust into the
holsters.

The other man was small, fat and cherubic-looking. His face
was smooth, pink and looked as if it never felt the touch of
a razor. A frank, open face, which would make people
like it. His chubby figure was encased in a sober black suit,
his white shirt plain and the bow tie knotted carefully. Dusty
Fog looked at the small man with more attention than he

might warrant. With eyes long used to searching, Dusty looked for some signs of hidden weapons: a wrist holstered Derringer, shoulder-clipped revolver or even a short-barrelled revolver in a coat pocket.

"What happened here?" asked the small man, his voice mild and high pitched.

A man who had been watching everything from along the street answered. "I've never seen anything like it, Mr. Rangoon. That *hombre* there," he indicated Smith's body, "started it. Went for his gun before either of these two made a move. The tall gent got him before he even cleared leather."

"That doesn't even answer my question. I asked what caused the shooting," replied Rangoon, looking at Dusty and Mark.

"They stole our pard's horse," Mark explained, eager to be on his way and discover what had happened to the Kid.

An angry rumble of sound came from the crowd at the words. Every man, be he cowhand, nester or townsman, agreed on how to treat a horsethief. In a country where a horse was the sole means of transport and to be left afoot meant almost certain death there was only one thing to do with a thief: kill him and do it fast.

"How do you know it is your friend's horse?"

Mark growled deep in his throat, sudden anger rising. The Ysabel Kid might be laying out on the range, badly wounded and needing their help; this was no time to delay in looking for him. There was an edge to Mark's usually even drawl which would have warned a man who knew him.

"Did you ever see a cowhand who didn't know his pard's horse when he saw it?"

"We can all make mistakes, young man," replied Rangoon, trying to look severe; though his face did not lend itself to severity. "I have four white horses in my ranch remuda, but I could not say if this is one of them or not."

"Hold hard now, Mr. Rangoon," a grizzled old cowhand put in. "I don't hold with that. I ain't seed your remuda but a couple of times, but I'd stake my thirty years' gatherings I'd tell this white from your'n or any other. I'd bet there ain't three whites as good as this'n through the West."

Dusty was still watching Rangoon, wondering what the man's motives were. He might try to look, talk and act like the greenest Arbuckle ever to come West, but some instinct warned Dusty the small man was far from the dude he appeared. It might be civic pride and duty which made him act in this manner, or there could be some more serious motive to it.

"I'll give you that I don't know much about horses, Turk," said Rangoon, turning to the cowhand with a benevolent smile. "But this is a peaceful town. We've never had a killing here. If we let one go unchecked we'll have the town blowing wide open. I would like these two young gentlemen to stay for an investigation."

Dusty's elbow rammed hard into Mark's side, stopping the heated words before they began. Mark was getting set to throw Rangoon through the window of the saloon and that would not help their position. Keeping his voice even and trying to hide the anxiety he felt, Dusty answered:

"Mister, our pard might be laying out there bad hurt, we're going to find him—and we're going right now."

"But . . .!" began Rangoon.

"There's no buts about it," growled Mark, before Dusty could say another word. "We're not staying here whittle-whanging while Lon dies."

"Watch your mouth, cownurse!" the gambler growled. "If Mr. Rangoon says you stop—stop you do."

Dusty looked at the gun which came into the gambler's hand, then at Mark. His voice was still even as he said, "Mister, we're going to look for our pard. When we find him we'll come back."

"Hold it!" The gambler's voice rose a shade. "I've got the drop on you."

"And right behind you," answered Dusty, "is a man with the drop—on you."

"Yeah?" scoffed the gambler, amused at the thought of any man trying such an ancient trick on him.

"Yeah!"

The voice came from behind the gambler; a cold, drawling sardonic voice he knew well. The speaker was a tall, slender man with a savage, wolf-cautious look about him. His dark, tanned face was at odds with the gambler's dress he wore, speaking more of long hours riding under the sun, than sitting at a poker table. The gunbelt around his waist showed the same excellent workmanship as Dusty's and Mark's. A pearl-handled Colt Civilian Peacemaker was butt forward in the holster at his right side, mate to the gun he held in his right hand.

"What's the game, Wes?" asked the gambler, not lowering his gun.

"You owe me a hundred dollars, Banjo. I wouldn't want to be collecting it off your body. This here's Dusty Fog and Mark Counter."

Once more talk welled in the crowd, for all the men knew those two names as well as they knew the identity of the man who spoke them. Most of the crowd were looking at Dusty, trying to reconcile his reputation with his appearance: that was how Dusty struck people when he first met them. Rangoon was looking him over with undisguised interest, although the gambler, Banjo Edwards, was inclined to scoff at the idea. Then Edwards realised that Wes Hardin was in deadly earnest and put his gun back into leather: that was policy when dealing with a man like John Wesley Hardin.

"What happened, Cousin Dusty?" asked Hardin, giving his gun a casual, spinning flip which ended with the Colt in leather.

"These two brought Lon's horse in. Allowed they took it from him."

Hardin growled a curse. The Kid was an old and trusted friend. "Get on and look for him, Cousin Dusty."

Dusty was about to go when he saw the expression on the faces of some of the crowd. He was grateful for his cousin's help but it did present a problem. Hardin was known as a real fast gun, a killer; the thought of him helping Dusty and Mark was making people suspicious, Dusty knew he could not leave Hardin holding down the crowd at gunpoint. Wes Hardin could do it, there was no doubt about that, but he might have to kill someone. Dusty did not want that, his cousin was not wanted for anything in New Mexico and Dusty did not wish it to change. There was one sure way of proving he knew the big white stallion.

"Tell you what we'll do, mister," said Dusty, looking at Rangoon. "One of you go lay a hand on the horse."

Rangoon shook his head. "I'm afraid I'm not much of a hand with horses. I'd best let Banjo do it."

Banjo Edwards stepped from the porch and walked towards the horse, hand reaching out. Nigger snorted, then reared up on his hind legs, hooves slashing down at the man. Edwards jerked backwards out of range and the horse lunged for him, only halted by the rope around its neck. One of the onlookers laughed.

"That's one hoss you can't handle, Banjo."

Dusty waited until Edwards was back out of the way, then stepped from the sidewalk, walking towards the big horse. "Easy now, Nigger hoss. Easy, old hoss."

The big white snorted again, watching Dusty with the angry eye-rolling which it showed every living person but the Kid. He went forward, never hesitating, speaking all the time. He knew the slightest indecision would bring the big stallion lunging. At best, Nigger tolerated Dusty and the other members of the floating outfit; only the Ysabel Kid could handle the white with impunity. For an instant Dusty expected trouble, then the ears pricked and he knew he was safe; Nigger recognised him. Dusty slipped the rope from the white's neck, then reached for the rifle in the saddleboot.

"There's a plate on the butt of this Winchester. It reads, 'Presented to Loncey Dalton Ysabel. First Prize. Rifle Shoot, Cochise County Fair'."

With that Dusty drew the rifle from the boot, offering it butt first to Rangoon. The Winchester was one of the magnificent "One of a Thousand" model 73's, the barrel chased and engraved, the woodwork finest black walnut. There was a tarnished silver plate set in the butt and Rangoon read the inscription. The small saloon-keeper nodded in agreement. There was no need for this proof, the horse had supplied enough.

"I'm sorry about this, Captain Fog," he said, raising his voice so all the crowd could hear him. "Of course, a gentleman like yourself realises how careful one must be. You know how easy a town can get a reputation for being wide open."

"I know," answered Dusty as he slid the rifle back into the saddleboot. "We'd best get moving."

"Certainly. You've showed commendable self-control. You must be anxious to go and look for your friend. Banjo, I'd like to see you inside."

With that Rangoon turned and walked back into the saloon. Banjo Edwards stood for a moment but Wes Hardin spoke:

"Sure, Banjo—so would I."

It was an order, not a request. Hardin was making sure

that the gambler neither followed nor attempted to stop Dusty
and Mark. Edwards had got away with it once, he would not
do so a second time. If he tried, either Dusty or Mark would
kill him. Banjo Edwards might think he was fast with a gun
but Wes Hardin knew either Dusty or Mark could take him.
Wes Hardin was fast, many claimed him to be the most
deadly and efficient killer of all; but he knew there was one
man who could draw against him—and walk away. That
one man was Dusty Fog. Hardin was one of the men who
knew how fast Mark was; faster than Banjo Edwards would
ever be. Hardin also knew that while the town approved of,
and would stand for, the killing of a couple of horse-thieves
it would not accept the killing of a local man; particularly
if the man worked for the popular owner of the Banking
House saloon.

Dusty Fog and Mark Counter did not wait to see what was
happening, they turned to head for the livery-barn and their
horses. Blinky Howard saw them returning and cursed himself
for a slow-witted fool. He should have guessed who they were
from the start. He had been a witness to most all that
happened along the street and had made a fair guess at the
cause of the shooting. Turning on his heel he went back into
the barn and waited. Dusty and Mark came in, the big cowhand leading the white horse.

"How much do we owe you, friend?" Dusty asked.

"Settle with me when you come back, Cap'n," replied
Blinky.

"All right, we'll leave our bedrolls here until we get back."

Dusty and Mark worked fast, saddling their horses. Blinky
stood by and let them get on. Finally he spoke. "Don't take
no offence at Mr. Rangoon, Cap'n. He's a real nice lil feller—
just not used to our ways. He don't mean no harm." Blinky
paused as if trying to make a decision. "I'm a man who minds
his own business Cap'n Fog. Allus have been. So I ain't saying a thing about them being a couple of hired guns who've
been hanging about in town here for a few weeks now. And
I ain't saying nothing about seeing them and six more riding
out. Headed along the Gunn River towards the nesters."

Dusty inclined his head. "Thanks for telling us."

"I never told you nothing, Cap'n," corrected Blinky. "I
minds my own business, like I told you. Hope the Kid's all
right."

35

"So do we," Dusty replied as he swung afork his paint. "Turn Nigger loose, Mark."

The big white stallion stood snorting for a moment, then set off from the livery-barn, headed in the direction it had been brought to town. The two men rode out after it, watching all the time. Nigger was moving definitely, not just running blind. Dusty turned in his saddle and looked back towards the Banking House saloon. Men were carrying bodies towards the undertaker's establishment. Dusty never took killing lightly, or liked doing it, even though he had been compelled to do so since he was fifteen. This time he felt less badly. The men were hired killers and must have cut the Kid down without a chance of his fighting back. All too well Dusty knew the Comanche-wild way the Kid could fight; those two could not have taken his horse while he was alive.

Something was worrying Dusty. The two gunmen might, or might not, have known who the Kid was. They would take his horse along, for a fine animal like the white would command a fair price. They should have kept the horse out of sight for a time for such a fine-looking animal would attract attention. The men would not head for the first town, or should not have done so. Then Dusty recalled how the two men had reacted when challenged; one stood and fought while the other tried to run away. Dusty puzzled this out, trying to keep his thoughts from the Ysabel Kid. There was not much of a chance that the Kid was still alive but Dusty knew he must go and see. If more than the two men were involved in the shooting, Dusty and every other member of the floating outfit would never rest until they were caught and killed.

The big white horse was sticking to a trail, following it with decision. The trail was nothing more than the scars left by the wheels of wagons and ran parallel to the Gunn River. About a mile from town the range changed into farming country: the occasional small house or brush encircled, cultivated land the small areas of growing crops protected from the range cattle. This was the first time Dusty and Mark had traversed the Gunn River country and they did not know the lay of the land, or the situation. They could see the nesters were there to stay but not in any great number; nor in a way which would affect the free range grazing of the ranches.

A small, rickety buggy came toward them, driven by a thin, workworn woman; a tired-looking man by her side. The man

36

looked up, saw the two cowhands coming towards him and reached down to lift an old Ballard rifle from the floor of the buggy. His eyes were cold and unfriendly as he watched them approach, following the big white horse. The two young men did not even glance at the buggy as they rode by, their only concern was to find their friend. The man turned as they passed him and watched them. Dusty and Mark did not look back, to do so was an insult, implying the person could not be trusted.

Further on, Dusty and Mark got another inkling of the situation in Gunn River County. An old man was working on a strip of land, following a big old mule as it dragged the plough. The man reached down and took up a muzzleloading rifle when he saw them approaching, standing with it held across his body. He did not relax until they had gone by. At any other time this would have interested Dusty and Mark; given them something to talk about. Now they were too busy with their own thoughts.

The chances of their finding the Kid alive were not great, yet neither could believe he was dead. He was their friend, but more than that; he was like a brother to them. It did not seem possible that he could be dead; would no longer ride the range and share their fun. They were thinking of the good times they had shared. Now they were going to look for his body.

They came over a rim and brought their horses to a halt, looking down at a small, neat house, then at the broken gate in the picket fence and the dead horse which lay outside. A buggy, with a patient horse in the shafts, stood by the dead horse but there was no sign of people. The white was going faster now; this must be the place where the Kid was shot, although they saw no sign of his body as they headed down the slope and brought their horses to a halt by the buggy.

A rifle barrel emerged through the window of the house, lining and cracking; the bullet slashing the air between Dusty and Mark. They reacted with speed: both were used to such things happening. They left the saddles and took cover behind the buggy, guns in hand. Dusty started to move when a second bullet hit the side of the buggy and a scared female voice yelled:

"Keep away, you murderers! Don't you come here!"

"Murderers?" Dusty spat the word out. "Lon's in there, Mark. I'm going . . ."

Mark caught Dusty's arm and hauled him down by sheer strength. "Easy, that gal's so scared she might hit you by mistake." He indicated the hoof-churned ground. "This's where it happened, looks like there was a bunch of them. I wonder how they got Lon mixed in with it?"

"Lon's dead," Dusty answered, hardly hearing a word his friend said.

Mark nodded, not wanting to speak about it. The girl in the house must know how it happened, but she would not let them get near enough. He shoved his gun back into leather and growled:

"That's a Springfield she's using. She can't get both of us."

"Sure," agreed Dusty, knowing what his friend meant to do. "Let's go!"

In the house Lindy Mahon stood by the window, resting the heavy rifle on the sill and rubbing her shoulder where the recoil slammed the steel butt plate against it. She had seen the white returning and the two riders following it. They were not part of the bunch which had attacked the house, but they were after Loncey's horse. With that in mind Lindy went into action without a word to her mother. She grabbed the rifle from the wall, dug out a box of bullets and started to shoot.

"What is it, dear?"

Lindy turned and found her mother standing behind her, face pale and worried. "Two men after Loncey. I've . . ."

What she saw stopped the girl from saying any more.

Dusty and Mark erupted from either end of the buggy, vaulting the picket fence and sprinting across the garden; separate, and swerving as they ran. High-heeled cowhand boots were not the best footwear for running but the two cowhands made good time. They had to confuse Lindy so she did not know which target to take first. They did just that.

Lindy's rifle swayed to and fro, first at Mark, then at Dusty. The girl could not make up her mind what to do and both men were coming closer all the time. Her finger tightened on the trigger and sent the bullet kicking up dirt between the young men. Desperately she jerked open the breech, it was stiff and she used all her strength. The extractor tore the head off the cartridge, a common and deadly defect with the Springfield; dangerous because it left the remainder of the cartridge case firmly fixed in the breech and rendered the rifle inoperative. Lindy stared down, not sure what to do. The two men were at the side of the house now, flattened on either side of the door.

Dropping the rifle she turned and darted across the room, taking the Pettingill revolver from the holster. She ran along the passage, facing the door and gripping the gun in both hands. The Pettingill was hammerless, a double-action weapon and it took strength to draw the trigger back. She lined the gun on the door as the handle moved, then jerked the trigger, tilting the barrel of the revolver up and sending the bullet into the wall over the door.

"What the hell's going on, gal?" asked an irascible voice.

A big, burly man came from the end bedroom. His brick-red face was angry though partially hidden by an enormous moustache. He advanced on the girl shambling along like a huge bear.

"The men who shot Loncey have come back, Doc," explained Lindy, pointing to the door. "They're outside now."

"Are they now?" Doc Bohasker growled. "Give me the gun, gal. I'll drum up some business."

Lindy did not argue, but handed the gun over for she knew Bohasker could handle it better than she. He hefted the Pettingill with some distaste and then strode towards the door, the girl following on his heels.

Dusty and Mark had reached the house and were flattened against the wall on either side of the door. They had seen the rifle leave the window and knew what might have happened. There was a chance they would get in and talk with the girl without being shot.

From inside the house came the flat crack of a light calibre revolver. Then behind them, Dusty and Mark heard the drumming of hooves and a voice.

"Hold it right there!"

They turned to see two men riding through the gate and up the path. The shorter of the pair must have been the one who spoke for he held a Winchester rifle across his saddle. He was a stocky man in range clothes, a county sheriff's star on his calfskin vest. He rode with a cowhand's grace, afork a good horse. The quality of his clothing showed he was an honest sheriff in a poor county. Around his waist was a gunbelt, a fighting man's rig and the old 1860 Army Colt in the holster showed signs of use.

The other man was taller, slim and mild-looking and rode a tired horse. He was a poor nester, a man trying to wrest a living from an unfriendly land. It was he who spoke:

"What do you men want here?"

"Our pard's been hurt, his hoss led us here," answered Dusty, moving forward. "The lady inside won't listen any."

The farmer looked at his house with worried eyes. He'd seen the dead horse and the blood on the path and now this cowhand was talking about a wounded friend. It did not make sense to him. "But what happened? What is that dead horse——?"

"Don't ask us," replied Mark grimly. "We came up just now, that hoss's been dead a piece. The lady started in to shooting as soon as she saw us and won't let us talk any. If our pard is in there we want to know about him."

Brick Hollister, sheriff of Gunn River County, kept his rifle on his knees, lining it without conscious effort on Mark. He gave Mark his full attention, making a basic and very dangerous mistake. His was disregarding Dusty Fog and it could cost him his life. He stiffened slightly as he heard the sound of a gun cocking on his other side.

"Boot the rifle, sheriff!" Dusty ordered.

Hollister looked across Mahon at Dusty, noticing the stance and wondering how he could have made such a fool mistake. "Go ahead and use it. If you reckon you can get me before I down your pard."

"Don't aim to try, sheriff. I'll holster my gun if you boot the rifle."

Hollister thought this over fast. He had made a bad mistake in dismissing the small man. That gun was held in the hand of a master. Hollister knew the small Texan did not need to call the play this way; the sheriff would have been dead without even knowing what hit him. So Hollister made the wisest decision. He slid the rifle back into the saddleboot.

"All right, let's have some talk."

At that moment the door of the house was thrown open and Bohasker came out with Lindy on his heels. She saw the sheriff sliding his rifle away and panic hit her. She grabbed the revolver and lunged forward, jerking it from Bohasker's hand, yelling:

"Father, these men attacked us and shot the young man who tried to stop them."

Mahon was a peaceable man, but no coward. He did not know what his daughter was talking about, but acted. Leaning over he started to jerk the long-barrelled Army Colt from Hollister's holster. At the same instant Lindy started forward, the Pettingill revolver swinging round to line at Dusty Fog.

CHAPTER FOUR

The Trouble With Trouble

BRICK HOLLISTER gave a startled yell, hand slapping down at his side as he felt his gun being jerked from his holster. But he was too slow to prevent Mahon drawing the old Army Colt. Dusty Fog was moving with the speed which made his name a legend. He was in close as Mahon started to swing the gun around towards him. His reaching hands caught Mahon's boot, jerked it from the stirrup then thrust upwards. Mahon gave a yell as he lost his balance and let the gun fall. He grabbed at, and missed, the saddlehorn, then fell, kicking his other foot free and breaking his fall with his hands. Even as he landed Mahon saw the small Texan picking up the gun.

Lindy lunged forward, the old Pettingill ready for use, meaning to protect her father. Mark Counter's left hand shot out from the side of the door, gripping the chamber of the revolver and twisting it, preventing her firing. Then with a quick pull he plucked the gun from her hand. His right hand went down, came up again, the ivory-butted Colt lining on Hollister.

"Hold right as you are, sheriff!"

Hollister froze, bending forward with hands scant inches from the butt of his rifle. He stayed still, very still, knowing that there was another good man with a gun. He also knew

42

that many a gun as good as either of the pair would have downed Mahon as soon as he made that stupid move. That they did not, warned Hollister that all–was far from being as it appeared on the surface. These two Texans were no trigger-fast hired killers, for if they were both he and Mahon would be dead right now.

"Keep still, all of you!" snapped Dusty, moving to jerk the rifle from Hollister's saddleboot. Now he and Mark held all the visible weapons.

Lindy stared at the rifle and revolver Dusty held, then at the Pettingill in Mark's hand. She realised that they were now unarmed and at the mercy of the two grim young men. The Ysabel Kid's old Dragoon revolver lay on the sideboard in the living-room, but it was empty. She felt ready to break down and sob, they were in the hands of two men she had tried to shoot.

It was Bohasker who broke the deadlock, moving forward and ignoring the Colt in Mark's hand. "Reckon you don't aim to use that gun, friend, so put it away. If you'd been fixing to kill any of us you'd have done it by now."

Mark's long-barrelled Colt spun on his finger, dropping back into leather. He turned and smiled at Lindy. It was a smile which charmed kisses from girls and food from cooks from Texas to Montana and back the long way. Reversing the Pettingill, Mark held it out to the girl.

"Here, ma'am. I hope I didn't hurt you when I took it. I don't like these hammerless guns, a man never knows when the trigger's far enough back to fire them."

"Now let's have some sensible talk for gawd's sake!" Dusty snapped, handing Hollister the rifle and revolver. "We ran across two men in town, they'd got our pard's horse and we wanted to know why. So we turned ole Nigger loose and he brought us here. Then somebody started shooting at us and wouldn't let us talk. That's why we came in like we did, tried to get near enough to make talk without being shot."

Lindy saw the big white standing with the other two horses and remembered something the Ysabel Kid had told her.

"Loncey said he was going to meet two friends in town. You must be the two."

"Why sure," agreed Dusty, then nodded to Mark as he walked back along the path to the white, reaching out a hand to stroke its neck. Dusty went on, "I reckon Lon warned you not to touch his hoss, there aren't many ole Nigger'll let do it."

"He told me that," Lindy smiled, relief flooding over her.

"If you look in his warbag you'll find a Colt Dragoon," Dusty went on, "one of the Third Model, with the detachable canteen-carbine stock. There's a plate in the butt that reads, 'To Mason Haines from his good friend, Jethro Kliddoe'."

The others looked at each other now, knowing a tragedy had been averted only because the two Texans knew how to control their emotions and tempers. They did not need further proof of the connection between the two Texans and the man in the house. Lindy was sure they were the friends her guest was meeting in Escopeta. They were so much like Loncey, slow talking, polite, yet terribly swift in action. She had thought Loncey was fast, but not when compared with the small Texan. There was one more proof, she decided, no stranger could guess the white horse was called Nigger.

"Yes, you are his friends."

"Yes'm!" answered Dusty. Mark was back by his side now and silent. Dusty hoped his friend would do the talking.

Mark did not speak. His throat felt as if it was blocked and his usually glib tongue stilled. He did not dare ask the question which seethed in his mind, but neither he nor Dusty dared hope the Kid was still alive, not after the way the girl had spoken when they arrived. The Kid was dead, they were both sure.

At last Dusty drew in a deep breath. His fingers worked spasmodically by his side, his face set grimly. "Is he——?" Even now he could not bring himself to finish off the sentence.

"No he ain't," replied Bohasker huffily. "I might not be a halfway good doctor, but when I get to them in time they mostly live."

It took some seconds for Dusty and Mark to understand what was said, to understand what it meant. Then a relief almost too great to bear flooded over them. The Ysabel Kid was not dead after all: he was alive. With an ornery old cuss like Lon that was all that mattered; give him anywhere near a fighting chance and he would come through.

Mrs. Mahon advanced from the passage where she had been watching. "He's badly hurt, but he'll live."

"Yes'm," said Dusty. His face showed the relief he felt and he sighed. "Can we see him, please?"

Mahon got to his feet, shaken by the fall and still confused. He looked around him, then asked, "What's been happening here? What horse is that out there?"

His wife ignored the questions, she was watching the faces of the two young Texans. Both were under a considerable strain, worrying over their friend's fate. It struck her in that moment how lucky her husband was to still be alive. Many men, particularly when as fast and efficient as these two, would have shot Mahon down and never given it a second thought. Even two such pleasant-looking men might, under the strain, have lost their tempers and acted without thinking. She knew the best way to ease the tension.

"Come inside, all of you. There's a lot to tell and from the looks of these two they need a seat and a cup of coffee before we tell it."

Dusty and Mark looked at each other, seeing the signs of the strain they had both been under. Dusty suddenly felt as he had the time he spent over three days continuously in the saddle dry-driving a trailherd.* He was tired and exhausted but managed a smile.

"How bad is he?"

"Not another word until you've taken a cup of coffee!" Mrs. Mahon interrupted. "Let's go inside."

Dusty was a cowhand; he thought of his horse before his own welfare. "We'll tend to the horses if you don't mind, ma'am. And bring Lon's gear in the house."

Mrs. Mahon spent the time explaining to her husband and the sheriff what had happened. Hollister listened to the story without a word. He was thoughtful, wondering what was behind the trouble in the Gunn River country. Then when Dusty and Mark returned, the party went into the house. Mahon led the way to the living-room and the men sat around. Hollister tilted back his chair, resting it on the back legs as he studied the two young men, wondering who they were. One thing he knew for sure—they were more than just fast with their guns: they belonged to that magic-handed group known as top-guns. He was willing to go further and say they were the fastest he had ever seen and quickly ran his mind over the descriptions of such wizards of the tied-down holsters as Ben Thompson, Clay Allison, Bill Longley, Jim Courtright or Bass Outlaw. None of the descriptions fitted

* Told in FROM HIDE AND HORN

45

either of these two young men. Neither one could be Wes Hardin, for Hollister knew who "Mr. Johnson" in town was. There was the Rio Hondo gun wizard, Dusty Fog, the big man might be him, except that Dusty Fog used the cross-draw. Hollister's eyes went to Dusty's guns, noticing how they lay, butt forward. That was how the Rio Hondo gun wizard wore his guns, but a small, insignificant boy like this could not be Dusty Fog.

The coffee was cowhand style, thick, hot, strong and sweet. The Texans drank the scalding brew with relish. Mrs. Mahon waited until they had finished, then opened the door and smiled.

"Come along and see your friend now."

Dusty and Mark followed the woman from the room. Lindy, not wishing to miss anything, swooped along the table, cleared up the cups, took them into the kitchen and then followed her mother. Bohasker looked up with an annoyed grunt, but allowed the two cowhands into the room. He growled a warning that they could not stay long and moved back.

The Ysabel Kid lay in the bed, clean sheets drawn up to his chin. His face was pallid under the tan, but the pain was gone and he might have been asleep. His clothes lay in a tidy pile on a chair by the bed, his gunbelt hung over the back, the holster empty and the knife still sheathed.

"That young cuss should be dead by any fair means," growled Bohasker with some satisfaction ."The bullet hit him in the body, glanced off his ribs, made a real bad tear and broke the rib. He'll live, his kind's too tough to die of something as simple as a broken rib. Lucky I was over to the Temple place, handling a confinement. Heard the shooting and came over."

"Thanks, Doc," said Dusty, gratitude plain in his voice. "You get him on his feet again and I'll cover any bill you want to put in. Not that he's worth a cuss one way or another, but we've had him around so long we've got used to him."

"Say," put in Mark, he had been looking at the empty holster and was puzzled. "Where's Lon's handgun? They didn't tote it off with them, did they?"

Mrs. Mahon shook her head. She watched the way the two men tried to hide their feelings for the boy. They must have

46

been suffering the tortures of the damned not knowing what had happened to him. Now, even more than before, she saw how lucky her husband was to be alive.

"No," she replied, "they didn't take the gun. We brought it into the house and I left it in the living-room."

"Pity," grunted Mark. "I thought we'd seen the last of that damned relic."

The Ysabel Kid's preference for his old, four-pound, Colt Dragoon revolver was a standing joke with the other members of the floating outfit. It was one of the square-backed trigger-guard, Second Model, made around 1850, and was superseded by the Third Model Dragoon, the 1860 Army model, various conversions by Richardson or Thuer to fire metallic cartridges and by the 1873 Model P., Colonel Sam's fabulous Peace-maker. Despite all the developments, despite the advantages metal cartridges gave for ease of loading, the Kid clung to and swore by his old Dragoon. He frequently declared, and proved, the Dragoon's reliability and man-stopping power.

"I think we'd better leave now," Mrs. Mahon said, catching Bohasker's sign. "He mustn't be disturbed from his sleep."

"That's right. Sleep's what he wants," agreed Bohasker. He was looking at Dusty and wondering who the small Texan was to speak with such authority about meeting the bill for the treatment of his friend.

Mrs. Mahon followed the Texans to the living-room again. Hollister watched them come in but did not speak. He tilted himself further back on the chair legs in his favourite way of thinking. Over the years he had learnt to tilt a chair to some amazing angles without falling over backwards. He was a strong believer in thought before speech and was turning everything over in his mind. When the time came he would be ready to ask any questions he thought necessary.

Mark asked Mrs. Mahon if he could fetch the Kid's saddle from where he had left it at the door. She took him out and Dusty went to the sideboard, picking up the old Dragoon. Setting the gun at half-cock he rolled the cylinder under his thumb and checked the chambers. The gun was empty, that meant some of the other men were dead. The Ysabel Kid might speak disdainfully of pistol shooting and boast of being a poor shot, but he could hit his mark when he needed to do so.

Mark brought in the saddle, laying it carefully on one side, then took the bedroll, opened it and removed the powder flask, bullet bag and roll of cleaning gear. Joining the others at the table he started to clean the old Dragoon, handling it with a care that his earlier scoffing did not warrant.

Lindy picked up the old rifle and looked down at the open breech. Dusty saw the expression on her face and joined her. "What happened, the usual?"

"Usual?" inquired Lindy, looking puzzled.

"Sure, the extractor ripping the head off the cartridge. That's the usual thing goes wrong with the Springfield." He told her, "Fact being, along with the stupidity of their leader that's what cost Custer's command their lives. I'll dig out the burnt case if you'll promise not to shoot it off at me again."

Lindy's face reddened, then she smiled, realising Dusty was only having a joke. Mark looked up from the gun, studied the girl for a long moment, frowned and said:

"Know something? This's the first time a *daughter* ever took a shot at me—at least, it's the first time one took a shot at me on my way in."

"What happened here?"

All eyes turned to Hollister as he spoke. His deliberations were complete and he was ready to get information. Mrs. Mahon told him the story for the second time, going into everything she could think of. The men sat in silence, all could imagine the scene. One man facing eight, and fighting them off.

"Why'd you say Lon was dead?" inquired Dusty, turning to Lindy when her mother had finished speaking.

"I didn't know you were his friends and wanted to keep you out of the house. So I called you murderers to make you think you'd killed him. It wasn't such a good idea, was it?"

"It was a smart idea," growled Mark. "You near on scared Dusty out of three years' growth."

"You said there were eight of them, ma'am," Dusty put in, bringing the conversation back to the shooting. "Lon got two, wounded another. We saw another two in town, leaves three more of them."

"Them two in town," interrupted Hollister, "they both dead?"

"Man'd say that's how they finished," Mark agreed. "They

48

tried to kill Dusty and me. What should we've done, stood by and called their shots for them?"

"One thing's for sure, though," Dusty put in, before Hollister could make a reply. "One of them knew who we were, or at least, guessed."

Hollister was wondering who the small man was and why he should think anyone would know him. "How'd you know that?"

"The way he acted. The other man stood and fought and he wasn't better than fair with a gun. The one I downed, turned and ran for it. But when he came round shooting he showed he *was* better than fair. Yet he ran instead of fighting. I reckon he guessed who we are."

"Which same's more than I do."

"This's Mark Counter, I'm Dusty Fog. The man in the bedroom's the Ysabel Kid. I reckon the gunman in town knew it. That was why he tried to run without fighting."

That figured to Hollister. Most any man would run if he knew he was faced with a shoot-out against Dusty Fog and Mark Counter. Far more so when the man was in possession of their friend's horse and thought that he had killed the Ysabel Kid.

"You say one of them was hurt, ma'am," remarked Mark, turning to Mrs. Mahon and receiving a nod in reply. He spoke to Bohasker. "I'd take it kind if you'd let me know when somebody comes in with a bad leg wound, Doc."

"Hold hard there!" Hollister said as he realised what Mark meant. "I want the men who did this."

"So do *we*!" Dusty's words were soft and gentle; but there was nothing soft or gentle about the set of his jaw.

"Not in my county. Four killings in one day. That's not going to happen again."

"Meaning?" Dusty asked.

"I'm not having any more trouble in my county."

"Mister," Dusty's voice was still low and menacing, "with trouble, it's people who don't want it who mostly get it. Like these folk here they didn't want none but it came to them. Or would have, happen Lon hadn't been here. Comes to that he didn't want it either, but he got it. Eight lots of it. There's three more lots riding the range now. Likely they'll be back to finish what they started here and ole Lon's in no shape to

49

handle them. Sure you have them—*if you get them afore we do."*

Hollister brought his chair legs crashing down to the floor and rose to his feet. "You can't take the law into your own hands. You've both held badges and know that."

"The law doesn't come into it, one way or another," snapped Dusty, letting the Springfield rifle slide to the floor and watching the sheriff. No longer did he look small, somehow he appeared to tower over every man in the room. "Lon's closer than any brother to us. He's stuck by us through anything we ever tied into and never worried about breaking the law. Now he's been cut down by a bunch of hired guns and we're not going to stand by until you get up off your tired butt-end and see what the hell's going on in your county."

Hollister and Dusty stood face to face, eyes locking in a struggle for mastery. Hollister was no Earp-style trail-end bully or hired fast gun, but a brave, honest and straightforward lawman who had made a few so-called hardcases back water. This time he knew he was faced with a man who was no blustering imitation. There was no bluff about Dusty Fog; he was supremely confident in his skill and his ability to handle any eventuality.

The situation was getting out of hand. Hollister was not the sort of man who could back down and hunt his hole. Neither was Dusty Fog. Lindy watched the two men, then moved forward, coming between them. For the first time her mother realised that Lindy was a grown woman.

"Stop it! Stop it! Both of you! The way you're acting would be better suited to a couple of saloon loafers than grown, responsible men. You've both the same idea in mind and want to get the men who attacked us."

Suddenly Dusty tilted his head back and let laughter burst from him. The transformation was amazing. He was once more the small and insignificant cowhand. The tension left him as he moved back a pace, his face flushed and red as he realised what he was doing. Dusty recalled the many times he had told his hot-tempered cousin, Red Blaze, not to act without thinking and to quit letting his temper run away with him. Now Dusty himself was doing just that. He was allowing his emotions to run away with his judgment. He grinned, if Cousin Red got to hear about it, Dusty was going to be rode unmercifully.

"I'm sorry, sheriff," said Dusty with a smile. "Reckon we were both sort of set to go off half cocked. Sure Mark and I'll be looking for the men who downed Lon. You couldn't expect us not to. If we can we'll bring them in alive."

"That's fair enough with me, Cap'n Fog. Reckon we both started to paw and bellow for nothing." Hollister replied. "I reckon having Wes Hardin in town's got me all shook up."

"Why?" asked Mark, grinning at the worried look on the sheriff's face.

"I don't know. All he's done so far is play poker—but he might be fixing to rob the bank."

Dusty laughed. "I don't know who's been telling you about Cousin Wes, but one thing he never does is rob banks."

Hollister stared at Dusty. "Cousin Wes?"

"Nor trains, or stagecoaches comes to that," Dusty went on without bothering about the sheriff's interruption. "Nor even people, unless it's with a mean deck of cards. All Wes's wanted for is shooting a nigger. 'Course, I know that's about as bad a thing as a man can do—even if the nigger was twice as big as Wes, mad drunk and coming in with a razor ready to use. That's what Wes Hardin's wanted for. They called it Reconstruction, but what it meant anyplace south of the Mason-Dixie line was if he's black he's right."

The Mahons and Hollister were not Confederate sympathisers but they knew something of the horror called Reconstruction in the south. It was a terrible period, fortunately now over, when the Union Army occupied the Southern States and protected the freedom maddened negroes. John Wesley Hardin shot down a huge, drunken negro who was trying to kill him with a razor and since that day was a hunted, wanted man, force to kill time after time to save his life.*

"So he's kin of your'n?" said Hollister, for he had never connected Ole Devil Hardin with the deadly Texas killer. He could foresee trouble ahead for the men who had shot down the Ysabel Kid. Dusty's next words proved it.

"Sure—and a real good friend of the Kid. Cousin Wes'll likely be on the look-see for the men who downed Lon. You want, I'll tell him to bring them in on the hoof."

"How'd he find them?" Hollister asked worriedly, seeing his peaceful county faced with a dangerous upheaval in the near future.

* Told in THE HOODED RIDERS.

"Man can learn a whole lot just sat in a poker game. Like I said, I'll pass Wes the word I want the men alive. That way we might just get them like it." Dusty's voice showed that if Hardin found the men first, there was not much hope of their being brought in any way but feet first. "We'll be staying on in town until Lon's back on his feet. I hope you don't mind if we drift in and see him regular, ma'am."

"Feel free," replied Mrs. Mahon. "I'm sorry for the way we all acted when you rode up."

"Shucks, ma'am, you'll be having us think you meant it next," Dusty replied and took up the Springfield rifle. "I'll fix this for you, then we'll head for town and send Uncle Devil a telegraph message, that we'll be delayed. He wouldn't want us to go back until Lon's on his feet. When'll he be ready to make some talk, Doc?"

"Not before tomorrow morning at the earliest and I don't want him disturbed much even then."

Mark finished cleaning the old Dragoon gun. Reaching across the table he picked up the powderflask and prepared to load the weapon. The powderflask had a measure fitted to the top that regulated the flow of powder and gave the correct forty-grain charge without the trouble of weighing. Mark tilted the flask over the top of the first empty chamber and pressed the lever, allowing the charge to flow in. Then he took up a round lead ball and placed it on top of the charge, turned the chamber under the rammer, worked the lever and thrust the ball home.

"Got me some combustible cartridges in my saddlepouch," Hollister remarked, watching Mark reach for the powderflask again. "I can let you have some if the Kid's out."

"No thanks. Ole Lon likes to pour her in raw and stick a round lead ball on top, then ram home. He allows that for man or bear there isn't a made cartridge and shaped bullet to touch that load."

Dusty, knife in hand, looked up from where he was carefully working the torn case from the breech of the Springfield. "Times are I agree with him."

The case emerged and Dusty laid the rifle on the hooks again, looking at it with disgust. Then his attention went to the Pettingill Navy revolver which Lindy had put back in the holster.

"Are these the only weapons you own?"

52

"Yes, Cap'n," Mahon apologised. "We never needed any-thing better and they were all we could afford at the time."

"They good enough for you?" Dusty inquired.

"We've never needed weapons before," Mahon pointed out.

"Man, you've got a whole lot of faith in Apaches. Was I you I'd get a repeater and a cartridge Colt. Had Mark and I been Apaches coming across that garden it'd have gone bad for your ladies."

"Cap'n Fog's right, Thad," Hollister went on. "If you can afford them I'd get a couple of decent guns. We've never had trouble with the Apaches, since they went on the reservation, but you know what Juan Jose's like. Give him but one good chance and a few rifles and he'll be off the reservation looking for war."

Mahon knew the truth of this. The chief of the reservation Apaches would be willing to dig up the hatchet and go to war. In that case the Mahon house would be poorly defended. It might never happen, but if it did, there would be no time to run for town and buy new weapons.

"We need the guns all right," he conceded. "Lindy, you go in and buy them."

Dusty drew the Pettingill, examining it. There was none of the wonderful, hand-fitting feel of the Colt about it. The Pettingill would be awkward to use, hard to keep in order and difficult to point by instinct. Then he was aware that this was not one of the .44 calibre Pettingill Army revolvers he had seen, but a .36 Navy model.

"I'll give you ten dollars for this gun. Uncle Devil collects firearms and doesn't own a Pettingill Navy. Reckon we owe him something for staying away from work, waiting for Lon to recover."

"That's good of you, Captain," Mahon replied, seeing there was no charity meant in the offer. The money would be useful, going towards paying for a second-hand cartridge revolver.

"Shucks, I'll take it out of Lon's pay when we get back home."

Lindy looked delighted at a chancce to go into town. Mahon realised for the first time how lonely it must be for the girl here on the farm. It was only on a rare trip into town she could meet up with people of her own age. The trip would do her good.

Mrs. Mahon was not so sure. "Do you think you can get to town and back today, dear?"

"You can spend the night with us if you can't, Lindy," Hollister put in. "My gal was saying she hadn't seen you for a piece now."

"We'll ride in with you," said Dusty. "I can telegraph Uncle Devil, fix up a room at the hotel and we'll bring you back in the morning. I'm wanting to hear what Lon says about the men who shot him."

CHAPTER FIVE

Bushwhack Lead

MILITARY AVENUE looked much the same as when Dusty and Mark rode out, except that the crowd was gone and the town lay under the heat of the sun at just gone noon. A spirited little black mare stood hipshot in front of Culver's General Store. A fine-looking little animal, probably some cowhand's go-to-town horse, Dusty thought as he tied his paint next to it. It was not a remuda horse for no mares were allowed in the remuda, but could be the sort of mount a cowhand would choose to come to town on, dainty and pretty enough to satisfy his demand for such things.

Lindy looked surprised to find herself in town so soon. The ride in went by without her knowing it. Mark drove the buggy for her, his big bloodbay stallion fastened to the rear. The sheriff and Bohasker left them at the edge of town and now they were at the store. She almost felt sorry that the ride was over for none of her friends had seen her with the handsome Texans by her side. There was a smile on her face as she looked at the little black mare.

Mark climbed down from the buggy and dropped the weighted rope which was fastened to the horse's bridle. Then he went around and helped Lindy down, before going to the rear, fastening his horse to the hitching rail and joining the others on the porch.

The inside of the store presented the usual mixture of goods that any small town establishment showed. The shelves, counters and boxes were filled with a wide variety of goods, almost anything a family would need for a home on the range. The stock ranged from needles to farming gear, from clothes to cooking utensils. The firearms were on a rack and in a glass-toped case at one side of the room, a fairly representative selection for the day, ranging from a couple of new Remington Creedmore rifles to an old muzzle-loading flintlock.

There were only two people in the store, a scrawny man behind the counter and a small, very pretty girl on the customers' side. The girl turned and her face lit up in a warm, friendly smile as she saw Lindy. For her part, Lindy was obviously just as pleased to see the girl, her delighted face showing they were old friends. This was further proved by the way they greeted each other.

"Hey shorty!" Lindy greeted.

"Hey fatty," smiled the other girl, her teeth contrasting with the tan of her face. "I was wondering if you'd show in town today—So was Brother Tad."

The girl looked pointedly at Dusty and Mark, seeing they were with Lindy. She knew Lindy's father was a nester and the two men were no sod-busters. They were cowboys, both of them and top hands at that or she had never seen one. They were looking back at her with the same interest. She was small, petite and very pretty, her dark hair cut almost boyishly short and very curly. Her clothing was ranch style, the shirt a violent tartan which jarred the eye, her skirt divided for easy riding and hanging just to the tops of her high-heeled cowhand boots. A low-crowned Stetson hat lay on the counter by her hand.

"Before you swell up and burst with impatience," Lindy spoke mockingly. "I'd better present my friends. This is Mark Counter and Dusty Fog—Boys, this is Mary Simmonds; she's colour blind, which accounts for her wearing a shirt like that!"

"Hey now, easy there, fatty," answered Mary, not showing any offence at the words. "I wouldn't want to tell the boys about the time you and Annie Hollister got drunk on applejack."

"I just bet you wouldn't," agreed Lindy, "seeing as how you was just as drunk as we were."

Mary Simmonds shook hands with the two young Texans. She did not know if she should believe they were Mark Counter and Dusty Fog. The cowhand was an inveterate joker and the two might be joshing Lindy, pretending they were two famous Texans. Then Mary remembered what she had heard on her arrival in town, looked down at Dusty's butt forward guns and knew the truth. Mary was born and raised on a cattle spread and could have told Lindy things about the two Texas men. She recalled the cause of the shooting in town.

"Did you find out what happened to the Kid?"

"Sure!" Mark agreed. "He'll live, thanks to Miss Lindy and her mother."

"Lindy and her mother," gasped Mary, swinging round to face her friend. "How did you get mixed in with the Ysabel Kid?"

Lindy did not get a chance to reply for the man behind the counter had finished checking through a list on a sheet of paper and looked up. "Got it all, Mary. I'll have it ready for your cook. When'll he be here?"

"Tomorrow morning, Pappy, Tad and our foreman are coming in this afternoon. Should be along any time now," Mary replied. "Say, Lindy, how about seeing the rest of the girls and stirring up a dance? We can take Dusty and Mark along."

"I'd like that," said Lindy delightedly, then her face fell. "Perhaps Dusty and Mark want to get back and see how Loncey is getting on."

"Shucks no," answered Mark. "Ole Lon won't be able to talk today and he's an obliging cuss. Wouldn't want us to miss a dance."

The girls exchanged glances. An impromptu dance at the livery barn would not be hard to organise and the other members of Escopeta's younger set would want to meet the two famous Texans. It wouldn't do Lindy or Mary one little bit of harm, specially to be seen as friends of Dusty Fog and Mark Counter. It might even make Mary's brother, Tad, just a little bit jealous, Lindy thought, which wouldn't be a bad thing at all. Then Lindy remembered why she'd come to town.

"I'd like to buy a revolver and rifle, please, Charlie."

"Take a look at them over there," the scrawny man answered. "They're all we hold in stock right now."

Lindy crossed the room and looked into the glass-topped case where the revolvers lay. There were a couple of new Colt Peacemakers on one side of a partition, on the other side, a half dozen or so secondhand weapons. Lindy sighed, eighteen dollars was more than she could afford to pay for a new revolver. She opened the lid of the case but hesitated. The secondhand weapons were where she must look but she did not want to buy a dud which would need a lot of repairs. Her eyes went to a pearl-handled Colt Artillery Peacemaker; it appeared to be the best gun of all in the secondhand section.

A hand reached by Lindy and lifted the revolver out. She turned and found Dusty by her side. He had seen the girl's hesitation and came to help her select the weapon for he knew the danger of buying a secondhand revolver. He turned the gun over in his hands, looking at it. He drew back the hammer, checking how it felt, shook his head and delivered his judgment.

"Was I you I wouldn't buy this one. It's been worked on by a would-be gunfighter. The safety notches have been filed level and the hammer spur checking removed. Look at the way these screw heads are bushed out. That means the man who made the alterations didn't know much about guns. You'd have trouble with this, was you to take it."

Dusty replaced the gun again and took out another. The pearl-handled Colt was a flashy-looking gun but not for someone who did not know how to handle a weapon worked on for extra speed. The hammer spur would slip from under the thumb with ease, that was why the checking had been filed off. The trouble was it might slide free at the wrong moment, firing the gun before the handler was ready.

The second gun was all right in appearance but a test showed that the chamber was loose. It was not serious yet, but would shoot looser until the gun became inoperative and needed costly repairs. The third gun was discarded when Dusty's keen ears and sensive fingers detected a gritting which told of dirt in the internal mechanism. It was something an experienced man could correct, but the Mahons did not have the experience.

"How about this one?" asked Lindy, indicating a Smith and Wesson.

"Looks all right, but I'd take me a Colt, was I you. The Smith and Wesson's accurate, real accurate, but it's delicate.

Needs too much care and attention to keep it working. Take a Colt Peacemaker now—you can drop it, bust up near on half the working parts and it'll still fire. Let's try this one."

Taking another gun he checked it over. The gun was made in the cheapest finish but it was mechanically sound, the working parts clean, the barrel rust-free and unpitted, the ejection rod and spring working and the chamber firmly aligned. He handed the girl the revolver and closed the lid.

"Let's see if I can get lucky and pick you out a rifle that works."

Lindy stood back willingly for she was in the presence of a master. Dusty's knowledge went far beyond handling and keeping guns clean, he knew them as a gunsmith would. Mary came to join her friend and watch Dusty pick the best of the three Winchester rifles in the rack.

"Is it as bad as all that, Lindy?" she asked.

"It could have been. Loncey stopped the first bunch. If they come back papa wants to have a decent rifle on hand."

Lindy accepted Dusty's choice, paid for the two weapons and a supply of ammunition then checked her money. She found that, by doing without a new dress she could afford a double-barrelled shotgun her father wanted. She had often heard him express his regret at not being able to afford a shotgun for the range held a plentiful supply of prairie-chicken and wild turkey.

"What now?" Lindy asked as the two Texans carried her purchases out and placed them in the back of the buggy.

"Go round to the Hollister's and leave the horses," Mary answered. "Then we can——"

Mary's voice trailed off. She stared along the street and all the colour drained from her face. The others looked in the same direction and saw two riders coming into town. Lindy gasped, paling as she recognised them. Dusty and Mark could tell that something was bad wrong. It was not the fact that the horses were running at a good speed, that was nothing out of the ordinary when cowhands came to town. It was the way they rode ,one hanging forward over his saddlehorn and apparently lashed in the saddle, the other bending forward, gripping the horn and swaying from side to side.

"Dusty!" gasped Mary, "it's my brother and our foreman."

The horses were running at a fair speed and the man did

not appear to be able to control them as he swayed from side to side. The second horse was fastened by its reins to the swaying man's saddlehorn and following him. Dusty and Mark leapt forward, into the street, fanning out so the horses could not get by them. It was Mark who lunged out and gripped the reins of the swaying rider's horse, bringing it to a halt. Dropping the reins he jumped forward as the rider began to slide from his saddle. The man was a tall, craggy-loking old-timer and no light weight but Mark braced his powerful legs and took the full weight in his arms. He carried the man to the sidewalk with no more effort than if he had been handling a baby, then turned to see if Dusty needed any help.

Dusty started to unfasten the ropes which held the unconscious rider in the saddle. They had been tied hard and it took him a couple of minutes to get them free. He caught the young rider and Mark lowered the old-timer, then jumped back to lend a hand. The stocky, young rider was lucky, there was blood on his head, another inch to the left and the bullet would have spread his skull's top wide open. There was a second bullet hole, just over the hip, but the bleeding had stopped from it.

Mark took the young rider's weight and carried him to the porch, laying him down by the old-timer. Dusty was by his side, looking down. The old-timer was barely conscious and would not be able to answer questions unless they were asked quickly.

At a time like this Dusty acted like a trained lawman. He found a crowd gathering fast, coming from the eating house and the two saloons. Mary and Lindy were on their knees by the side of the two men and Dusty gave his orders fast.

"All right, back off there, all of you. Come on, make room. *Pronto!*"

There were big men in the crowd, men who towered over Dusty but not one of them thought to argue about his orders. They might not know who he was but they knew *what* he was —he was not the sort of man one argued with when he gave orders in that tone of voice.

Mary bent over the old-timer. "What happened, Hank?"

"They bushwhacked us, gal. Get the sheriff," the old man croaked out the words in agony. "Got your pappy."

Mary stiffened and Lindy gripped her arm, lifting her to

her feet. The ranch girl was pale and stood rigid. There was no hysteria in her face, or tears, yet, the reaction would set in later. Dusty gave Lindy a grateful glance for the last thing he wanted right now was a grief-stricken girl on his hands. He took charge of the situation.

"Go fetch the sheriff, friend," he snapped to a cowhand, then to a nester, "Fetch the doctor. The rest of you keep well back. Any of you ladies know anything about handling bullet wounds?"

A middle-aged woman stepped forward. "I help Doc with his work."

Doctor Bohasker came fast, he had been on his way for an after-lunch drink when he got the word. The crowd scattered from his path like cowhands avoiding a fresh-branded steer. At a time of emergency Bohasker was likely to kick any man who got in his path out of it again. He stalked forward, nodded his approval when he saw the way Dusty was handling things, then looked down at the woman.

"How is it, Jenny?"

"Not good. Both of them've been hit hard."

"All right," Bohasker barked, seeing there was no need for him to make any temporary treatment in the street. "Get them down to my place. I'll need you along with me, Jenny."

The old-timer was trying to sit up, his leathery face working in agony. "Lemme get up—I've got to get after that bunch—They downed the boss!"

"Lay back here, damn you to hell, Hank," growled Bohasker. "You're not fit to ride any place. Where the hell's Hollister?"

"Coming now," answered Dusty for he had seen the sheriff approaching at a run. "Can I talk to the gent?"

Bohasker might have snarled out a refusal but he knew who Dusty was. His eyes went to Mary, seeing the rigid way her face was set. The girl was holding herself in control as he had expected she would. "You can have a couple of minutes, Cap'n. No more. I'll get men ready to help carry them down to my place."

"Where'd it happen, friend?" asked Dusty, bending over the old-timer.

Hank Strong looked up and even in his pain recognised Dusty for what he was. "They was lined on a rim three mile out of town. Got us as we rode by. Never gave us a chance."

"See who did it?"

"Nope. They must have hid up there and started to shoot as we went by. Got the boss first, then hit me 'n' young Tad. Managed to get Tad clear—roped him to his hoss and got him here."

"Any idea what they were using?" Dusty asked for he knew there was a considerable difference in the sounds made by Winchester and heavier calibre rifles.

"Heard a Sharps first, that's what got the boss. Then Winchesters."

An angry rumble sounded from the crowd, or from the cowhands in it. The Sharps rifle was something few if any cowhands carried; it was too long, awkward and heavy calibred for their needs, so they mostly carried the shorter, more compact repeating-fire Winchesters.

"Ain't no call to go blaming the nesters!"

Dusty straightened up, turning to discover who was speaking. Banjo Edwards and Rangoon stood in the forefront of the crowd. The gambler met Dusty's eyes for an instant then looked away, making no attempt to comment further.

It was too late. The cowhands in the crowd were growling angrily as they heard the words. The nesters in the crowd moved close together and the cowhands began to bunch. There was danger in the air which must be nipped in the bud before it could fan up into open hostility.

"Nobody blamed the nesters," Dusty's voice cut through the noise and brought it to a stop, *"except you."*

Edwards studied the small Texan for a long moment without saying a word. His frown deepened and he growled, "See you've come back again."

"Why sure, have you paid Cousin Wes yet?"

Edwards opened his mouth to reply but Rangoon brought his elbow round, slamming it into the gambler's side. This might have been an accident and was done so fast as to pass unnoticed. Dusty was the only man who, noticing the move, attached any importance to it. The others, if they thought about it at all, would have dismissed it as a simple accident. Accident or intention, the change in Edwards was immediate, the truculent attitude left him and he relaxed.

Mary stood with Lindy's arm around her shoulders. She looked straight at the gambler. "I'll never believe the nesters had anything to do with the shooting, Mr. Edwards. No matter what you say."

"Me?" shrugged Edwards. "I'm only saying what a lot of folks'll think."

Hollister came up at that moment, stopping any more talk. He looked at the two wounded men, then at Bohasker who shook his head. Turning to Dusty the sheriff asked for information. Quickly and without wasting words Dusty explained all he knew, allowing Hollister to form his own conclusions. The county sheriff's office was responsible for investigating the shooting. Dusty did not envy Hollister his task in doing so under the present circumstances.

"You'll want a posse, Brick," remarked Rangoon.

"Yeah, I'll want a posse," Hollister agreed, looking around the crowd at the mixture of cowhands and nesters. He could read the signs and knew that forming a posse from either group would cause resentment and trouble. If he took all cowhands the nesters would refuse to believe anything they learned; it would be the same if he took all nesters. Even a mixed posse would be no better for there would be doubt and mistrust amongst the members.

"Count Mark, Cousin Wes and me in, sheriff," said Dusty Fog.

Hollister was more than grateful for the offer. It solved the problem of who to take along. The three men were known for their skill with guns and would be more than a match for any gang they might meet.

"All right, Cap'n Fog. We'll get horses and head out."

"I'll go along with you, Brick," Edwards put in.

"It won't do any good, Mr. Edwards," snapped Mary. "Those three men won't listen to your trying to blame the nesters."

"What's that mean?" Edwards growled.

"Every time there's trouble in Gunn River County you start to blame the nesters for it. I've heard the hands at the spread talking about it."

Banjo Edwards growled under his breath. The crowd would remember what was said and how the girl defending the nesters was the daughter of a rancher.

The friendship between the two girls was a serious stumbling block to certain well-laid plans. Mary's father was the

63

most moderate of the ranchers. The other cattlemen, Colt Blayne particularly, would be less likely to keep the peace. Mahon was also a moderate man, not given to roughness as were the Rand family and some other nesters. However, the two girls were friendly with most of the people in their own factions and would be listened to before any violent action was planned.

"There's no need for you to come along, Banjo," Hollister replied, for he did not care for the gambler.

"I think it might be advisable, sheriff," stated Rangoon blinking mildly. "After all—with no disrespect to these three gentlemen—they *are* all cowhands, having the interests of the cattlemen at heart. It might be as well for an unbiased observer to be along. Not, of course, that I'm implying Captain Fog and his two friends would be influenced by personal bias—but you know how people think and talk."

Hollister was willing to concede the point to Rangoon. The small man knew how people thought and reacted in this kind of condition. The nesters would never be willing to accept that three men with roots so deeply embedded in the cattle business would play fair. Banjo Edwards was a man who might be termed neutral. The gambler worked in a saloon which drew trade from both sides of the county. It would not do the saloon any good to take sides in the trouble and Edwards was, in consequence, as near a neutral observer as Hollister could take along with the posse.

"Get your hoss then, Banjo," Hollister ordered. "And you, Wes."

Hardin turned, making for the livery-barn. His face showed nothing of the fact that he had been up all night playing poker and not managed to get to bed after the game broke up at eight-thirty in the morning.

The crowd left as the two wounded men were carried to the doctor's house. Dusty watched them go, seeing the way the two factions stayed apart. They were going about their busniess, apparently leaving the sheriff and his posse to handle things. The trouble would remain smouldering until the posse returned, then it would fade out—or burst into roaring flame.

A hand touched Dusty's sleeve and he turned to find the two girls standing behind him. Mary was still holding her emotions as best she could; her eyes were dulled with unshed tears and her lips were tight to stop them quivering.

"Dusty, pappy was bringing in some money to meet our note at the bank. I—would you—please——"

"Don't worry none, honey," replied Dusty gently. "We'll tend to it all for you." He pressed her arm, then went on. "You take care of her, Lindy. Take her to Hollister's and wait until we come back."

Edwards and Hardin returned with their horses and the sheriff's daughter brought his, saddled and ready. A thin, sallow-faced man drove up in a buggy, a man wearing sober black clothing. He was Hobart, the county undertaker and coroner, going along to help with the investigation. It was a grim-faced party which rode out of town.

"This's where we could use either the Kid or young Waco," growled Hardin. "They can both read sign like they made it."

Dusty agreed with this. The Ysabel Kid and Waco,* another member of the floating outfit, were experts at reading sign. Dusty and Mark could follow an easy line, but they were mere beginners compared with the others, to whom a few broken blades of grass told a story.

Dusty knew his own limitations at following a track and wondered if Hollister was skilled in sign reading. Most county sheriffs could read a certain amount, they needed to in their business. Dusty was willing to go along with Hollister in charge as long as the sheriff proved to be competent at his work. If the sheriff was to prove incompetent Dusty would feel free to go his own way.

There was little talking as the men rode along; they were alert and watchful for the men who did the shooting might be around. Hollister led the posse, keeping to the well-marked trail which led to the Simmonds' ranch. The trail ran along the bottom of a valley, the sides of which rolled up gently on each side. Turning a bend they came on the scene of the killing and brought their horses to a halt.

"This's where it happened," announced Edwards unnecessarily.

"Why sure," Dusty agreed, looking ahead. "There's only one thing wrong. The old-timer didn't tell us half of it."

"He didn't tell us there were two bodies here."

* Waco's story is told in the author's floating outfit books.

CHAPTER SIX

Banjo Reads Sign

THE POSSE swung from their horses. Hobart, the coroner, brought his buggy to a halt and climbed down, reaching for the bag which lay on the seat. The men waited for Hollister to make the first move but the sheriff did not go forward immediately. First he looked up at the top of the slope, trying to detect any sign of life which might warn him of danger. The men who had done the shooting might still be lining the rim, guns trained on them. His eyes flickered to the horse which stood with hanging reins near the bodies, then up to where, high in the sky, buzzards wheeled. The birds would not be there if men were on the rim. Already they went spiralling away as if knowing there would be no meal for them.

Drawing in a deep breath, Hollister said, "Let's take a look."

He walked forward with the men following him. Hollister knew one of the still shapes, and cursed for Walt Simmonds had been a good friend. The other body was a stranger to him.

Dusty Fog and Mark Counter were flanking the sheriff now. They were both trained lawmen and knew what to look for. The tall, grey-haired man would be the rancher, they guessed, that much was obvious from his clothes. He was laying on his back, his head shattered by the heavy bullet. Death would have been instantaneous, nothing was more certain. In the rancher's stiffened right hand was a Colt revolver, his holster empty. His pockets were turned out and his shirt ripped open. There was no sign of the money he was bringing to the bank.

The other body was dressed in range clothes, the holster hanging low and tied down. He was face up, the features twisted in an expression of agony; under the dirt and tan the skin looked unusually pallid. He had been shot at close range, in the chest, there were powder burns and singeing which told of a close-fired revolver, not of a long-range rifle shot. There was little blood on the wound in the chest. Dusty saw this, then he looked down at the man's right leg. The leg was a bloody horror of torn, lacerated flesh and splintered, mangled almost severed bone. The lower part was smothered in blood from knee to boot soles. There was no need to make a close inspection, few weapons made so severe a wound. A Colt Dragoon revolver, firing a soft lead ball with a full forty-grain charge would do so.

Hollister watched Dusty roll the body of the dead gunman over. The back was ripped open but there was little blood from the gaping hole. Dusty allowed the body to flop back to the ground and looked up.

"This's Simmonds," remarked Hollister, indicating the rancher's body. "I've never seen the other one before. He wasn't on the Lazy S crew last time I went out to the ranch. Simmonds' crew ran to younger men."

"Was I taking money I'd say he's the man Lon shot in the leg," Dusty drawled, watching the gambler's face.

Banjo Edwards was frowning, puzzled by finding two bodies. Then he saw what Jarman and Lloyd's bunch must have done. He kept his mouth shut, waiting to see what the others made of it and ready to steer their thoughts in the right direction. He also saw why Jarman came to town, and eyed Dusty grimly. The small Texan and his friends were spoiling all the carefully made plans.

"Not from me, you wouldn't," said Mark, twisting his face wryly. He had seen the Kid's pistol work before. "He's the one. Ole Lon's Dragoon sure tears hell out of a man."

Wes Hardin agreed with this for he also knew the damage the Kid's old Dragoon caused when striking bone. His eyes flickered to Banjo Edward's face, reading the trouble on it, his poker-playing training enabling him to catch signs which would have been invisible to less skilled men. He did not say anything, but his eyes were on the gambler as Edwards bent and lifted up the gun in the rancher's hand.

"Been fired once. Must have shot this *hombre* here."

"After being shot in the head?" Dusty inquired sardonically. "There's a man with guts."

"Could have been shot after downing this *hombre*," growled Edwards. "I know how it looks to me. Simmonds met up with this *hombre,* one of the bunch who hit at the Mahon place. Saw he was wounded bad and knowed he was going to need doctoring. Knew that Bohasker'd ask questions, then got rid of this jasper rather than take a chance on it."

"Then shot himself in the head, put lead into his son and foreman," Dusty scoffed, "all with one bullet."

"Hank said they were hit by rifles from up on the rim," Edwards pointed out.

The coroner was bending over the gunman's body now, looking at it with the cold disinterested stare of a man who had seen violent death many time. He stiffened slightly as he looked at the body wound. Dusty was watching and their eyes met. The coroner opened his mouth to comment on the state of the wound but Dusty shook his head. The coroner shut his mouth again and Dusty bent over, mouth near Hobart's ear.

"Not yet, friend," said Dusty, holding his voice down so that only the coroner heard him. "I've seen it, too. Let's see how the rest lays before we say anything about it."

"Simmonds was bringing money to town, sheriff," Mark said. "Looks like they cleaned him out."

Hollister searched the body, doing it with cold distaste. The pockets were turned out and he could find no money. "They cleaned him out," he agreed.

Banjo Edwards was prowling around, looking at the side of the slope. He stopped and bent forward to look at certain marks in the short grass. "Come down this way, fair bunch of them."

The rest of the posse gathered and looked at the blurred, indistinct depressions in the springy grass. All but one set of tracks were unidentifiable one way or the other. The clear set showed up; heavy, blunt-toed and low-heeled boots set well apart, showing the wearer was a tall man. Mark turned and looked at his own tracks, they were not leaving such a clear imprint in the grass. It was almost as if the man with the blunt-toed boots meant for his tracks to be read.

"Nester boots," said Edwards triumphantly.

That was plain from the sign. The cowhand, spending most of his time on a horse, wore sharp-toed, high-heeled boots and not blunt toes or low heels. They were the sort of things a man would wear for following a plough or any of the other nester tasks a cowhand would find *infra dig*.

"You sure about it?" Dusty asked mildly.

"*Sure?* Of course I'm sure. Look at them toes, them low heels. Did you ever see a cowhand with boots like them?"

"Can't say I ever have," agreed Dusty, eyes going to the blurred sign left by the other men from the rim. "Wonder how it's so plain and the rest's blurred?"

"They came down and went back on the same tracks, that's why." Edwards used the first explanation to come to him.

Dusty refrained from asking where the heavy sign went on the way back for it was only in view coming down, well separate from the rest. It puzzled him for a moment, then he got the answer. The man wearing the nester boots was big and heavy built, likely, but he should not, even with heavy stamping, leave such a plain track. With the extra weight of carrying the dead gunman across his shoulders the man would leave a clear print. Dusty started to tie things up with what he knew and what he suspected.

"Best get on and read some more sign for us, mister," suggested Dusty waving a hand to the slope.

Hollister opened his mouth to object, then shut it again. In the short time they had know each other, the sheriff had formed a good impression of Dusty Fog's ability and knew the small Texan did nothing without good reason. Hollister know Banjo Edwards was a gambler and rarely if ever went out of the saloon. It was not likely he would know anything about the mysteries of reading a track.

With eyes on the ground, giving a fair impersonation of a trailing buck Apache, Edwards went up the slope. The others followed him, also examining the ground but with more attention than was obvious. The crushed grass showed that Edwards made one correct guess. The men came down and went back on the one line. All except the one in the nester's boots who appeared to have only come down. There was no sign of the plain tracks going back up again.

69

There was more sign at the top of the slope. The grass was crushed down where several men lay. That the men waited some time was plain from the cigarette butts and a couple of cigar stubs which lay around, mingled with empty cartridge cases. Most of the cases were the short brass tubes of the Winchester rifle, but one Edwards picked up was almost twice as long.

"Sharps bullet case," he stated.

"Looks that way," agreed Dusty gravely. "Wonder why it was left."

"How do you mean? Why it was left?" growled Edwards.

"Just what I said, why was it left lying here?"

"It's been fired," snorted the gambler, "anybody can see that."

Dusty nodded in agreement. "Why sure, it's been fired—and left. Mister, Sharp shells cost good money. A man doesn't just leave them laying around. He takes them back to be reloaded. Why's this one lying here?"

"Couldn't find it, or didn't have time."

Dusty did not point out that the case lay in plain view all the time or that the man who had fired it found time to wait around and go down the slope to the dead rancher. "That could be it," he said, mocking disbelief in his voice.

The men fanned out to make a more careful search of the area. Now was the time Dusty found himself missing the skill of the Ysabel Kid. The young man would have read the full story here and been able to give a very clear picture of what happened. Instead they would just have to muddle along as best they could, with Mr. Edwards' invaluable assistance.

Mark made the next discovery; he moved along the top of the rim while the others fanned out, making for the small clump of trees which lay back from the top. His shout brought them to examine his remarkable find.

Near the edge of the rim some freak of nature left a grass-less, dusty depression in the ground. What caused this Dusty could not explain; he had seen similar things before and did not think anything about this one for it was not the cause of the dust patch which attracted Mark's attention.

At the edge of the patch, showing clear and precise as if placed in with some care, were the imprints of a pair of low-heeled, blunt-toed boots. Beyond them, with equal care, was the shape of a big burly man, the marks of his bib overalls outlined clearly.

"It *was* a nester then!" Edwards sounded triumphant at having his theories proved to *his* satisfaction. "I never yet saw a cowhand who'd wear bib overalls."

That was true enough. The cowhand would never wear shoulder-strapped bib overalls of that kind. They were the clothing of the nester and no self-respecting cowhand would be seen dead in them.

For all that, Wes Hardin appeared to be disturbed. "What I don't see," he grunted, "is why a man should lay here in the dust when he could have been in the grass with the others."

"Nesters aren't smart," scoffed Edwards.

"They're too smart for a damned fool trick like that," Dusty answered, he was studying the marks in the dust. The man must have stepped forward from his clear pair of tracks and got down with considerable care, pressing himself close to the ground, then getting up again with the same care. "Let's take a look at where they left their horses."

A quick search of the trees showed where several horses had been tied. They had been left for some time, from the droppings scattered around. Hardin went on through the trees and at the other side found where other horses had been fastened. He called the other men to him and showed the sign.

"Five hosses, one led without a rider," he guessed.

"What do you make of that, Cap'n?" asked Hollister.

"What lays over thataways?" Dusty asked, waving a hand in the direction the tracks approached from.

"The Gunn River and the nesters!" Edwards spat the words out. He was beginning to realise that the other members of the posse were suspicious. Those stupid fools, making sign as plain as that. It stood out clear, too clear, too obvious.

"That figures," Dusty agreed, his eyes went to the sheriff. "I'd bet there are a couple of bodies in the Gunn River, was a man able to check on it."

"Couple of bodies?" Hollister growled, his hackles rising at the thought of more killings in his county. "How do you mean?"

"The two Lon downed. Be the easiest way to get rid of them. Leave them out on the top of the ground and they'd get found. Bury them and the coyotes might dig them up.

71

Sink them in a good deep hole in the river and they'll likely never be found."

"That's right enough," agreed Hollister. "There's plenty of holes like that on the river."

"How'd you know they were the same bunch who downed your pard?" Edwards asked, watching Dusty with a grim stare.

"Easy, were eight of them. Lon got two, wounded one and killed a hoss. Left six men, seven horses. Two of the men came into town, leaving four, including the wounded man, and five horses. Sign shows that only four of the horses were carrying weight, the other was being led," explained Dusty. "They'd bring the horse along with them, must have been carrying a brand that could be read. Came here and joined the bunch who got Simmonds."

"But the bunch that hit Mahon's place were cowhands," Hollister objected.

"And this bunch here are supposed to be nesters."

Edwards growled out an annoyed curse which brought the attention of the other men to him. "You seem dead set on proving the nesters didn't do it."

"Near on as set as you are to prove they did," replied Dusty.

Edwards glanced at Mark and Hardin before facing Dusty, his fingers spread over the butt of his gun and his eyes locking with the small Texan's gaze. He was suddenly worried. Hardin was real fast, a man, Edwards knew, who could cover any bets in the shooting game the gambler might bring up. Edwards thought Hardin would move in and take his cousin's part, but he showed no sign of doing so. Rather, both he and Mark Counter lounged back with complete indifference as if they knew Dusty Fog could handle any move the gambler made. His eyes went to Dusty again and met the small Texan's own. Met them and read something in them which made him pause.

There was neither fear, nor indecision in the small Texan's grey eyes. Only the cold, complete confidence of a man who was real fast with a gun. Edwards thought of himself as a good man with a gun; he believed that there were few better. Yet, he knew that here stood one who was better. A man who did not think anything at all about it but *was* faster than Edwards ever would be. Slowly Edwards let his hand drop to his side, turned and walked away.

Hollister let his breath out in an audible sigh of relief for he knew Edwards and had expected trouble. "We'd best check on where they went, I reckon," he said.

"Looks as if they scattered," remarked Dusty. For him the incident was over. Banjo Edwards joined the ranks of those Dusty was forced to face down.

The guess was correct, the men separated, splitting up into groups of two or three men. Further away from the trees they scattered again, going off singly. The reason for this was obvious, as obvious as the sign at the other side of the trees. A large group of men travelling would leave a plain track. Individual riders would be far harder to follow. They would come together at some pre-arranged rendezvous, or else head back separately for their headquarters.

"How about trailing them?" Hollister asked.

"Depends on how good you are," replied Dusty, glancing at the tracks. "Mark and I aren't better than fair and I don't think Cousin Wes's any better."

"That just about covers me. I usually get young Johnny Brace from Blayne's spread," the sheriff admitted. "He's been raised by Apaches and can read sign."

'How about our friend, Mr. Edwards?" Mark inquired. "Reckon you could trail them, seeing as they aren't headed for the nesters?"

"Me?" Edwards snorted. "I can't read sign."·

"We'll make a try on one set, I reckon," Hollister ordered. "Try and see where they're headed."

Before they could make a move a shout from beyond the trees stopped them. "Sheriff! Hey, sheriff! Where are you?"

"Here, through the trees!" Hollister yelled back. "Who is it?"

"Lonegan, from the Eating House!" The speaker was shouting as he crashed through the trees. A townsman came into sight, running, face flushed with the exertion. "There's going to be trouble in town."

"What sort of trouble?" Hollister growled.

"Colt Blayne and the other ranchers are in town and most of the nesters," the man gasped. "Things are looking bad, they're all in the Banking House. Doc Bohasker's got his ten gauge out and he's sat in the middle of them. Got them on opposite sides of the room and says he'll give himself some trade if anybody makes a wrong move. He'll do it, too."

Hollister knew full well that Bohasker was capable of doing

just what he said. The doctor knew the danger of allowing the two groups to come together and was all set to prevent it. For all of that the situation was explosive and a wrong move on either side could blow the whole thing into the air. Turning to the posse he said:

"We'll have to leave it for now. Even if it does mean losing them."

"Sure," agreed Dusty, "this's more important than following a track and most likely losing it without getting anywhere."

"Some of us should oughta go after that bunch," Edwards objected.

"All right, you go," snapped Dusty. He knew Hollister was going to need all the help he could get in town and suspected Edwards knew it also. That was why the gambler suggested following the tracks.

"Doc told them you'd hold an inquest when you got back, Brick," the man from Escopeta told the sheriff. "They're holding off for it."

Hollister made his decision immediately. The murder of the rancher called for an investigation but the situation in town needed his attention. With feelings running high it would be easy for a spark to stir up a prairie-fire of violence. "We'll get back. It'd be dark before we could follow the tracks any place."

They returned down the slope and helped the coroner load his buggy with the pair of tarpaulin-wrapped shapes. Dusty helped the man fasten the ropes holding the bodies back whispered, "Don't mention about that feller until you get back to town and start the inquest."

"All right, Cap'n. I'll play it your way," replied the coroner. "This's real bad business."

"It's bad," agreed Dusty soberly. "Likely to get worse before it's done with. I hope Doc holds them apart till we've had a chance to talk to them."

A horseman came racing towards them. It was Blinky Howard, from the livery-barn, riding further than he had done in years. He brought his horse to a halt and almost before the dust had settled was giving his news.

'Rangoon stopped selling likker in his place and the cattlemen headed for the Gunn River but Frank done the same. There's some hard talk and they want you back in town as fast as you can make it."

Hollister mounted his horse, his face thoughtful. Then he turned to Dusty, Mark and Wes Hardin. "I need some special deputies, will you three take on. Could even use one regular, how about it, Cap'n?"

"One, or two?"

"One, this's a poor county."

"Then we're out. Mark and I want to work together until this blows over," replied Dusty. "And we don't want tying down with no law-wrangling chore until we find the men who shot Lon."

Turning to Wes Hardin the sheriff grinned. "Don't want to sound like I'm offering you seconds—even if I am, Wes. How about it .Will you be my deputy?"

Hardin grinned just as broadly. The idea of him, the most wanted man in Texas, being a deputy sheriff appealed to his sense of humour. It would be a new sensation to wear a lawman's star.

"Sure, I'll do it. Be pleased to help you out."

"I'll give you a badge and swear you in as soon as I get a chance. We've got to cool those hot-heads down first."

They rode in silence for a time, then Hardin remarked, "This's going to slow down you folks putting up Hantley's statue. A range war'd just about break the folks around here."

"Hantley?" asked Dusty. "You mean that Yankee colonel who was killed by the Apache Kid a couple of months back. The one who wrote his life story?"

"That's right," agreed Hollister proudly. "Escopeta was his home town. You know about him?"

"Why sure," grinned Dusty. "I read his book. Said a few nice things about the ole Texas Light in it."

"He sure did," scoffed Mark, having also read the book. "It made you act so high-toned we had to throw you in the hoss trough. Hantley was the man who lost all his men holding a house on the Cumberland, wasn't he?"

"That's right," said Hollister. The pride was even more in evidence now, pride in Hantley's achievement and the fact that he was an Escopeta boy. "He was a lieutenant then and him and his men held that house for three days, against two Confederate regiments. The relief found him wounded and every man he'd got in his command dead."

" 'Cepting one, way I hear it," corrected Dusty.

"Just some major from the Quartermaster Corps," snorted Hollister, waving aside the idea that anyone but Lieutenant Tom Hantley did anything towards defending the house on the Cumberland. "He didn't do nothing. It was good ole Tom Hantley who ran the whole shebang. That major got shot up some they reckon but it was Tom who ran the fight."

"Town's going to put up a statue to him," remarked the coroner. "He went right through the War without taking another scratch. Went up north against the Sioux and come through it. Commanded the fort over by the reservation, then went to Arizona Territory and gets killed by that murdering renegade, the Apache Kid."

Dusty lounged in the saddle, thinking of the wild days when he led his hard-riding company against the Union Army. He had heard of Hantley's defence of the house, not against two regiments, but a weak battalion. For all of that, it was no mean feat and one which brought rapid promotion to Hantley, carrying him to Colonel. Dusty regarded the man's career after the fight as being ordinary and not marked with any other brilliant strategy such as the defence of the house against a superior force. Being a soldier at heart Dusty could always find time to admire an enemy if he was efficient and brave. He held no views for or against Hantley, never having met the man. Dusty rode in silence, imagining the defence of the house and wondering who the major of the Quartermaster Corps had been.

CHAPTER SEVEN

The Inquest

ALL THOUGHTS of Escopeta's hero were forgotten as the posse came back to town. There was a brooding silence in the air which men who rode long with danger could feel and read. Military Avenue was deserted, looking like the main street of a ghost town as the nesters stuck to the Banking House saloon and the ranch crews stayed in the Gunn River saloon at the other end. No citizen of the town showed his or her face on Military Avenue; that would be like walking between two herds of buffalo as they charged at each other.

Hollister licked his lips as he rode along the deserted street. He looked at the three Texans who were to be his deputies and on whom he now relied to keep the peace. It was well to be backed by such men at a time like this, they were as good as a troop of cavalry. Even with them it would be touch and go if trouble was to be averted. Hollister paused, not sure what orders to give. He had never come up against such a situation before and did not know how to handle it.

"Reckon we ought to get a scatter each?" Hardin inquired.

Dusty shook his head. "No go, Cousin Wes. That'd be like waving a red flag at a bull. We'd best play it—" The words

77

died off as Dusty remembered he was not in command. "Sorry, sheriff. You tell us what you want doing."

Hollister was wise enough to know the small Texan was the best man to handle things. "I'll play it any way you say, Cap'n."

"All right." Instantly Dusty was giving his orders. "Mr. Hobart, take the bodies down to your place, then come back to the Gunn River and start the inquest. Mark, head for the sheriff's house and bring Miss Mary and Lindy back with you, if Mary can manage it. Wes, you go ask the nesters to come along to the Gunn River for the inquest."

"That's taking a big chance, isn't it, Dusty?" asked Hollister, using Dusty's name for the first time.

"Sure, so'd any other way of doing be. That's why I want the girls along. The men'll be less likely to cause trouble if the girls are there. I want everybody to hear what's got to be said. Who leads the two sides?"

"Colt Blayne, he's a Texan, speaks for the ranchers; owns the biggest spread and been here the longest. Big Hunk Rand's the one the nesters listen to and follow," Hollister answered. "Funny thing, I've seen Colt's boy, Sam and Silvie Rand around a few times, looks like they're going steady. Be hell on if either Colt or Big Hunk got to know."

The group separated, the two townsmen going to their homes, the Texans to follow Dusty's orders. Dusty found Edwards sat his horse watching everything. The small Texan turned and halted not more than three foot from the gambler. His voice was low and gentle, deceptive as the first whisper of a Texas blue norther storm.

"Mr. Edwards, you try and open your mouth in there before the inquest, either about what we saw—or what you want folks to think we saw—and I'll bend a gun barrel over your lil ole pumpkin head."

Edwards noted the continued use of the word, "mister" and remembered what was said about the sons of the Lone Star State. "If a Texan calls you mister once, he's curious. If he calls it you more than once, he just don't like you." Edwards was quick on the uptake, he got the idea. Dusty Fog did not like him.

"Yeah!" he growled, trying to sound savage and confident. "You reckon you could do it?"

"*You* reckon I can't."

78

Once more Edwards tried to meet Dusty's eyes and failed. He was beaten and knew it. Turning his horse he rode for the livery-barn, leaving Dusty the undisputed master of the field.

Dusty swung down from his horse and left it at the hitching rail, then followed Hollister into the saloon. The low rumble of talk came to a halt and all eyes went to them. Dusty looked around the room, he could tell the different ranch crews from the groups which were formed. The ranchers sat at a table to the right of the room. Colt Blayne was prominent; one Texan could always tell another. The rancher was a short, grizzled, but quick-looking man. His son, a tall, handsome blond cowhand, was by his side.

"This here town gone dry, Brick?" Blayne asked.

"For now. Until after the inquest," Hollister answered. "Get all your boys across the room to the right."

"Why?" growled Blayne.

"As a favour to me." It was Dusty Fog who replied. He moved forward to flank the sheriff and a low murmur went up from the crowd.

The cowhands moved, they guessed who Dusty was and no man was going to argue with *him*. The change of place was barely finished when the doors opened and Wes Hardin brought the nesters in. The hostility in the room hit with solid waves as the two groups faced each other.

If the nesters were not hunting for a showdown they managed to conceal the fact very well for every one of them wore a revolver or carried a rifle. They were led by a big heavy man who would have looked more at home in buckskins than in the dirty bib overalls he wore. He was Big Hunk Rand, a Kentuckian who came West to make a new life for himself. Across his right arm lay a Sharps Ole Reliable rifle, a .50 calibre weapon which was accurate to a mile.

The second man into the room was a picture of Big Hunk Rand when he was about twenty years old. He was as tall, heavily built and dressed in the same way, with a Sharps in his hands. This was Lil Hunk Rand, the nester's oldest son.

Dusty looked for Mahon but saw no sign of him. It was a pity for Mahon was a moderate man and would be a restraining influence on the others. The batwing doors opened and Rangoon stepped in; behind him towered Bohasker, a magnificent twin-barrelled shotgun under his arm.

"What the hell are the fodder-forkers doing here, Brick?" Blayne growled.

"When you gets to be County Coroner you can ask questions at an inquest, Colt," boomed Bohasker. "Until then shut and stay shut. And you, Big Hunk."

Rand's snigger died down, he went to a table, sitting at it with his rifle resting under his right hand. Lil Hunk settled on his haunches by his father, resting his back against the wall. Big Hunk watched the other nesters sit on the left side of the room, then his eyes swung to the cowhands at the right side. The doors opened and Mark came in with Lindy and Mary.

"What you doing, bringing gals into a saloon?" asked Blayne.

"Same as you, attending the inquest," Bohasker barked. "So shut your face. This Coroner's Court's going to be run peaceable one way or another."

"Gentlemen!" Dusty's voice cut over the angry mumbling of the crowd and brought a silence to the room. "I agree with Doc. The name is Dusty Fog and any man who doesn't agree with me, step outside and say so—but bring a gun."

The silence which followed Dusty's words could almost be felt. A whisper ran around the room, telling any doubters that the small Texan spoke the truth: he really was Dusty Fog. Big Hunk looked at the small Texan with interested gaze and Lil Hunk's eyes glowed with hero-worship for both were Confederate supporters, even with the war so long over. One thing they, and every other man in the room knew, Dusty Fog meant just what he said; he would kill any man who made trouble.

The threat, along with the presence of the two girls and backed by Doctor Bohasker's shotgun, brought peace to the room. How long it lasted would depend on how Dusty's views on the shooting were taken.

The coroner was in the saloon; he crossed to the bar and jumped up to sit on it. Bohasker joined him, resting the ten-gauge across his knees and looking mean as a starving grizzly bear.

"All right!" Bohasker boomed. "We're here to investigate the killing of a citizen of the——"

"We don't need no damned inquest!" yelled a cowhand, leaping to his feet. "It's them damned nesters who——"

80

"Sit down, Bell," said Rangoon gently, "or I will be compelled to fire you."

The cowhand sat down and Bohasker nodded his thanks to Rangoon while the nesters grumbled angrily. Banging the butt of his shotgun on the counter, Bohasker shouted, "One more interruption and I'll use this. Sheriff, tell us what you found out."

Hollister stepped in front of the bar, cleared his throat and began to tell what they had discovered. Dusty was pleased with this; it gave him a chance to watch the reactions of the crowd. The sheriff was telling everything just as it was, without any attempt to point out the things he must know were wrong.

An angry rumble came from the cowhands when Hollister told of the sign and of the plain marks in the dust patch at the top of the rim. The cowhands and the ranch owners acted just as Dusty expected them to, they looked at the one fact.

"Never saw a cowhand wear boots like that," shouted Colt Blayne.

"Colt!" Bohasker bellowed. "I ain't warning you again. Sit down and shut your face—or get out of here."

Blayne, face working angrily, started to come to his feet but his son caught his sleeve and held him down. Bohasker glowered at the rancher; they were good friends who drank, played poker, hunted and fished together. The doctor also hunted, drank, played poker and fished with Big Hunk Rand.

"There were two men, Brick," said Bohasker, when silence fell again. "Who was the other man?"

"A hired gun from the look of him. I've never seen him before and there was nothing on the body to identify him."

"How'd he been killed?"

"Shot from close up."

"Was that his only wound?" Bohasker went on.

"Nope. He'd been shot in the leg. Real bad wound."

"Could he have ridden far with the leg wound?"

"Not without help," answered Hollister. He could see the way the nesters were looking at each other; what had happened at the Mahon place was common knowledge. So was the fact that one of the men on the raid was wounded in the leg, badly wounded at that. Rand had called in at the Mahon place on his way into town and heard the full story.

"That'll be all, Brick. Stand down now," growled Bohasker,

81

then caught the sign Dusty made to him. "Captain Fog, you take the stand and tell your side of it."

Dusty moved to the front of the crowd, halting and hitching up his belt. "I agree with the sheriff on what we found. We saw those things and we were supposed to think such and such happened. The sign was plain, too plain. It was planted to stir up trouble between the nesters and the ranchers. That wounded gunny—sure, he was likely the one the Ysabel Kid wounded at the Mahon place."

"Then that means—" began a nester, but Rand waved him to silence.

"I know what it's *supposed* to mean," agreed Dusty. "It's supposed to mean Simmonds met up with the gunny, his man, saw he was bad wounded, daren't risk letting Doc there see him, and shot him down." Dusty ignored the angry growl from the cattlemen and Mary's gasp. "Then we're supposed to think a bunch of nesters saw what was happening and gunned Simmonds down. That sign in the dust patch, where a man lay down to line a rifle, was real convincing. It showed the man was big, heavy built, wore blunt-toed boots, used a Sharps and wore bib overalls."

"Showed all that did it?" Blayne growled.

"Why sure. Could see the mark of the top of the overalls *real plain*," Dusty said, then looked at Lil Hunk Rand. "You help me, friend?"

"Sure will, Cap'n Fog," replied Lil Hunk, uncoiling his long body and coming to his feet faster than any man ever had seen him move, unless there was a chance of hunting or fishing involved. "What you want me to do, Cap'n?"

"Come out here and get down like you was going to line a rifle."

Lil Hunk shambled forward, Sharps on his arm. In the centre of the room he went to his knees, and lowered himself forward. His left hand supported his body, he rested his right elbow on the ground and tucked the butt of the Sharps into his shoulder. The upper half of his body, including the top of his bib overalls, never touched the ground at all.

"Thanks," Dusty said drily. "Want any more men to get down and show you, gents?"

The men watched Lil Hunk get to his feet, they had all got down with a rifle at one time or another and saw what Dusty was getting at. There was no way a man could leave the mark of the top of his overalls unless he lay flat on his stomach.

Colt Blayne growled in his throat. "A big man with a Sharps, wearing bib overalls."

"That's right," agreed Dusty, "just like that."

"A nester?" Blayne went on, eyes on Rand.

"That's the way it was meant to look."

"Meaning me?" There was menace in Rand's angry drawl.

"That's the way it was supposed to look," answered Dusty, then turned to Blayne. "You're an intelligent man, Colt. Would you have laid out there some place that would show plain sign. Now would you?"

"Can't say I would."

"Then do you reckon this gent's dumb enough to do it? A mountain man, a man who knows about hunting and tracking. Would he make a damned fool play like that."

Blayne might be hard-headed and hot-tempered but he was a fair man and knew Big Hunk Rand. "Naw, I reckon not— Wait a minute. Blunt-toed boots? I never yet saw either Big Hunk or any of the Rands wear boots, allus moccasins."

"That's right," Hollister spoke up, face lighting with relief. "I've seen Big Hunk digging and wondered how the hell he did it with moccasins on. His feet must be like iron."

"We never had no trouble until them sod-busters come in," yelled a cowhand.

"Us nesters had trouble, too," came the reply from a nester.

"That's right, and you all know it," Mary Simmonds said, getting to her feet. Her face showed signs of her grief but her voice was under control. "You know it is, Uncle Colt. You sent Sam and the boys to help the Rands with a burning barn. Pappy had all our boys riding the river range to keep cattle from off the farmers' crops."

The girl's intervention placed a temporary damper on the tempers of the men, reminding them that ladies were present and any fighting might endanger them. Dusty was grateful to Mary for speaking when she did.

"The nesters have been around here for a piece now," Dusty reminded them quietly. "Yet the trouble only started three month or so back."

"How about them rifles that downed Walt Simmonds?" a rancher asked. "One of them was a Sharps. Brick says they found an empty Sharps case up there."

"And I got a Sharps," growled Rand.

"Only rancher who's got one is Colt and he was with me all day," replied the rancher.

"Sure Rand's got a Sharps," snapped Dusty. "So's my Uncle Devil and maybe two or three thousand other folks. You reckon ole Christian Sharps only made the one and sold it to Rand?"

"One thing, Cap'n," drawled Rand. "Sheriff allows that gunny with the leg wound couldn't ride far without help. Sheriff reckoned Simmonds' gun had been fired, what at?"

"The wounded gunman."

There was an angry roar at the words, the cowhands knowing how the nesters would see this and not liking the implication. For a moment trouble seemed to be certain but Dusty waved the men into silence and went on. "Sure, into the gunny and out at the back. There was hardly any blood at either hole."

"What's that mean?" Rand inquired. "Way I see it Simmonds knowed that gunny."

"What're you getting at, nester?" Blayne roared and threw back his chair.

"Hold it!"

Dusty's matched guns were out and lined on the rancher. Blayne stood still, hand gripping his gun butt, frozen by the fastest draw he had ever been privileged to see. The Rands were coming to their feet, swinging their rifles up but Mark Counter acted with a speed which almost equalled Dusty Fog's. The Rands found themselves looking at the muzzles of two ivory-butted Colts and remained still, their rifles only half raised. The cowhands found themselves facing Wes Hardin's Colts, and the nesters were held down by the combined efforts of Hollister's old Army Colt and Bohasker's twin-barrelled ten gauge.

The moves came so fast the crowd were taken completely by surprise. Every man thought the guns were picking on him personally as a target and so stayed rooted to the spot. Not one of them doubted that if the issue was forced the five men would shoot and friendship would not prevent them.

Even at that moment, Hollister found time to marvel at the speed with which Dusty, Mark Counter and Wes Hardin moved. He also realised how fast Mark Counter was. Hollister had thought Mark was just a good man with a gun, could never remember hearing the big Texan's speed mentioned.

84

From what he had just seen, Hollister knew Mark could be classed up there among the best, the top-guns: he was as fast as Wes Hardin and almost as fast as Dusty Fog.

"Sit fast all of you?" Bohasker's bellow rang out, as he jerked back the hammers of his ten gauge. "Damn it to hell, what's wrong with you. Snapping at each other like a pack of cur dogs."

"That's right," yelled the coroner. "Sure the bullet went through the gunman but that wasn't what killed him. He was dead before the bullet hit him. That was what Captain Fog meant about there being so little blood. The leg wound killed him, loss of blood and shock. Being bounced on a hoss didn't help any either. Walt Simmonds didn't even fire the shot, he was dead before it happened. I'm sorry to have to say it plain like that in front of you, Mary gal. But I've got to stop these fools before they start shooting at each other. That gunny was dead for at least an hour before Walt Simmonds."

"What do you make of it, Brick?" Blayne asked, sitting again.

The Rands settled down once more and the rest of the men took a lead from the heads of their groups.

"Let's listen Cap'n Fog out, shall we?" asked Hollister, waving his empty left hand, then dropped his Colt into leather.

Dusty holstered his guns again and relaxed. Then he looked at the men with annoyance and contempt plain on his face. "This was all part of a plan to set you folks at each others' throats and it damned near came off. Way I see it the killing of Mr. Simmonds and the raid on Mahon's place tie in. Mahon was to be taken to the place where Simmonds was killed and left there, made look like they'd fought and each hit the other. The Ysabel Kid spoiled that play. Mahon wasn't at home but the Kid was and he fought them off. He got two and wounded a third; the two are most likely at the bottom of the Gunn River. The wounded man was more use to them, so they took him along."

"How do you mean?" asked Rand.

"Easy, you've likely seen what a Dragoon does when it hits bone?" Dusty said and Rand nodded. "It put a mark on a man that can't be missed. That meant the gunny was a danger to them. They couldn't take him to a doctor without having it remembered. They knew that the wound tied the

85

gunny in with the raid on the Mahon place. Then they knew they couldn't carry out their plan of taking Mahon and killing him. So they took the gunny and left him with Simmonds. To make sure, they put a bullet into the gunny from Simmonds' gun. Now, happen you'd found them, what'd you think, Rand?"

"That Simmonds killed the gunny rather than have him took to a doctor. That he hired the gunny, then shot him."

"Which same's what you was supposed to think. The cowhands wouldn't believe it or accept it even if they believed it. They'd say all the sign pointed to nesters killing Simmonds. There'd be hard feeling build up and sooner or later some hot-headed young fools'd start in to shooting. There's not one of you'd likely have looked beyond the sign. You'd have painted for war and dug up the hatchet. Which same somebody wants real bad."

"And who might that be, Captain Fog," asked Rangoon mildly. "Do you suspect anyone in particular."

Dusty might have been speaking to the other men but he was watching Rangoon's face all the time. "Maybe."

"Would I be in order if I asked who you suspect?"

"One thing my pappy taught me, Mr. Rangoon. Always to keep quiet when I suspect something, only talk when I'm holding enough evidence to hand to the court," said Dusty. "You folks've all been living in Gunn River for some time?"

"Most all of us've been here for years," replied Hollister, frowning and wondering what Dusty was getting at.

"And the trouble started about two or three months back? Who's moved in to the county in that time?"

"Nobody, not permanent," Hollister answered.

"I only arrived here four months ago, maybe a little longer," interrupted Rangoon, coming to his feet.

"You?" Hollister laughed. "Nobody suspects you, Rangoon."

"We sure don't," agreed Blayne. "Do we, boys?"

There was a chorus of agreement at the words. The men in the room sounded as if all knew that Rangoon was above suspicion. There was a hint of condescension in the way the men voiced their opinion; the patronage of big men dealing with a small man. Dusty, watching the small saloon keeper all the time, saw the look of annoyance and anger which flickered for an instant on the mild face. None of the others noticed it.

"Let's get this thing finished with, boys," called the coroner, seeing that the men were thinking of what Dusty said and were settling down. There would be no trouble between the cowhands and nesters that day.

Colt Blayne came to his feet. "Been thinking, Brick. You could use a deputy, what with one thing and another."

"I could spare Banjo for a few days," remarked Rangoon, his face under control once more.

"Couldn't deprive you of him, Rangoon," said Hollister, knowing the saloon keeper liked to be called by his surname rather than his given name of Horace. "I've took me a deputy on. Mr. Johnson here."

"*Johnson!*" Rangoon's voice raised a pitch or so. "But he's——"

"He's what?" Hardin's voice was soft and gentle.

"Er—He's a good choice. It would be a brave man who'd make trouble in the county while Mr. Hard—Johnson wears the badge."

The rest of the men were in agreement with this and with Hollister's choice of a deputy. They knew Mr. Johnson and John Wesley Hardin were one and the same. They also knew Hardin's word was his bond and once he took the oath of office he would uphold it to the best of his not inconsiderable ability.

"That sets well with me," Blayne growled. "How about you, Big Hunk?"

"And me. Hardin's a good Texas name. I'll back him."

"One thing, gents," drawled Hardin, soft and threatening as the snarl of a crouching cougar. "If there's any more trouble, come into town and let us know about it. Just to please me. I'll thank the man who does—or doesn't."

The men set back their ears and listened real good. This was the man who made Wild Bill Hickok back water and caused other wizards of the tied down holster to sing low in his presence. Any request he made was likely to be listened to and acted upon. A man did not need John Wesley Hardin to raise his voice to know he meant every word he said.

"Will you take a drink with me, Hunk?" Blayne asked.

"Be pleased to, Colt," drawled Big Hunk. "There's a white-tail deer raiding my north forty, bigger'n a buck elk. Happen you got time come over and we'll take a whirl at bringing him in."

The coroner's court was forgotten now but its purpose achieved for it had stopped a bloody war breaking out. The two faction leaders were reconciled to the point where they could offer each other drinks and fix up a hunting trip. There would be no trouble in Gunn River County for a time.

The men gathered at the newly-opened bar or headed for the Banking House saloon which Rangoon gave orders to be re-opened even though he stayed on for the nightly poker game.

Dusty and Mark left with the sheriff and the two girls. On the sidewalk Hollister stopped, took out his bandana and wiped his face. There were times in the saloon when he had felt as if he was seated on an open powder keg and people were flipping lit matches at it. Things were close in there and not just the atmosphere either.

"Man, I wouldn't want that to happen every night. Come on down to my place, Cap'n Fog, and you, Mark. How's Tad and Hank, Mary gal?"

"They'll live, both of them," replied Mary, still holding her voice firm, but as he took her arm, Dusty felt her shivering. "Who could have done it?"

"I'm reckoning, not saying," drawled Dusty. "This thing's deeper than I first thought. When I've proof I'll make my move."

"Reckon Banjo Edwards is in on it, Dusty?" asked Mark, taking Lindy's arm.

"He's not smart enough to plan a thing like this. Straight shooting'd be his way. I don't reckon he's the big augur."

"Augur?" Lindy looked puzzled.

"Boss, the top man," explained Mark.

"Texas talk," Mary went on. "He's all the time trying to stir up trouble for the nesters."

"I've heard Lil Hunk Rand and some of the young farmers say Banjo blames the cowhands for everything," Lindy objected. "Do you think he's the one, Dusty?"

"Hell, Dusty, you must be funning," said Hollister before Dusty could make a reply. "Banjo works for Rangoon."

"So?"

Hollister laughed. "You'll be telling me you suspect Rangoon next."

"Couldn't be him, now could it?" Dusty's voice showed nothing of what he thought.

" 'Course it couldn't," snorted Hollister. "Look at him. Hell, a small, fat *hombre*. I never seen him pack a gun, don't reckon he'd even know how to use one. Him! Planning a thing like today. He's only a little man, don't stand no more than five foot six."

"Sure," agreed Dusty Fog. "I'm five foot five and a half myself."

CHAPTER EIGHT

Captain Fog Makes a Call

MRS. MAHON ushered Dusty Fog and Mark Counter into the small bedroom; the Ysabel Kid was conscious and awake. He lay back against the white pillows, looking pale and weak, yet there was something of the old grin on his face.

"How is it, boy?" Dusty asked.

"I've felt better. Hear tell you got two of them."

"Sure," drawled Mark. He sat on the edge of the bed and dipped a hand into the bowl of fruit on the small bedside table. Taking an apple he bit into it. "We'll get the rest of them before you're on your feet again. Then we'll head for home. Was I you I'd lay back and take it easy for a piece."

"Why?" asked the Kid.

"Ole Devil's going to love you for holding us up. He'll have you on the blister end of a shovel to get even."

The Kid watched Mark and Dusty help themselves to his fruit. "Hope there's worm in 'em. Say, Doc showed me the bullet, from a forty-five, he allows. Now that pleasures me no end."

"Why?" inquired Dusty, eating the apple and chancing there being a worm in it.

"Goes to prove what I've been telling you all along. A forty-five's no use as a man-killer. They don't get up when I hit 'em with my ole Dragoon gun."

"Did you know any of them?"

"Nope, none of them. Cheap hired guns every one. There wasn't a cowhand there. You'll know one of them, I hit him in the leg."

Mark finished his apple and tossed the remains into the bowl. "We found him. He's dead. Any more apples in there?"

"Huh!" grunted the Kid; eyeing the apple core, then his friend. "You can't take him no place twice. They won't even have him back to apologise for the first time."

Dusty laughed. It was good to see the Kid talking, even though he was far from recovered and in no condition to take care of himself. It was this thought which worried Dusty and had been since the previous night. Dusty and Mark ate at the sheriff's house, then spent the night at the small hotel in town. There was some talk and many theories discussed. Hollister still held that Rangoon was above suspicion and Dusty said nothing to dissuade the sheriff's beliefs.

The Kid twisted his head to look at the gunbelt which hung over the back of Dusty's chair. Mrs. Mahon left the weapons there, for the Kid was insistent about it and would not settle down. She did not want him to keep on fretting, so she hung the gunbelt close to his hand; Dragoon full loaded and bowie knife sheathed.

"Tell you, Dusty," said the Kid. "I don't like being this close to an Apache reservation and tied down in bed. I'll feel better when I can get to my gun and sit up with it."

"You lay back there and relax, boy," Dusty snapped. "Don't start fussing or fooling. Happen you do I'll tell Mrs. Mahon to hawgtie you."

"And I'll write Miss Juanita that you got all shot up saving a pretty gal," warned Mark. "She'll be down here painted for war."

The door opened and Mrs. Mahon looked in. "Time's up boys. Doc Bohasker warned me not to allow you to stay too long."

Dusty and Mark rose and went towards the door, then turned to give the Kid a final word of good cheer. "See you, Lon," said Dusty. "Behave yourself."

"Sure," agreed Mark, grinning. "Don't go away."

"I'll be here," promised the Kid, settling back again, exhausted by the effort of talking to his friends.

Mrs. Mahon took the two Texans into the living-room and waved them into seats. Mahon filled his pipe and then turned to the cowhands. "I hear the Kid saved my life yesterday. Big Hunk called in on the way back and told me about the inquest. You made quite an impression on both him and Lil Hunk. I'm sorry about Walt Simmonds, he was a good man."

"Is Lindy all right?" asked Mrs. Mahon.

"Sure, ma'am," Dusty replied. "She's staying on to take care of Mary."

"Told us to say she'd be going out to the Lazy S with Mary for a few days," Mark went on. "If that'll be all right with you."

"Tell her to stay as long as she wishes," replied Mahon. "Mary'll need a friend by her." He laid his hand on the butt of the shotgun which the Texans brought from town for him. The new rifle and revolver were on the sideboard, his eyes went to them. "I reckon we can take care of ourselves and Lon for a few days."

"We'd best head back to town then. Mark and I want to see if we can track down the men who shot Simmonds. Thanks for taking such good care of Lon."

Mahon smiled. He had never really known cowhands before but these two Texans were making him change his opinion about the reckless, hard-working, hard-playing sons of the saddle. "That's all right. He took care of us."

Dusty and Mark rode back to Escopeta. The small Texan was silent and Mark, who knew Dusty well, made no attempt to converse. There was something worrying Dusty and Mark knew when his friend had sorted it out he would talk.

They reached town in time to see the mourners leaving the graveyard after Simmonds' funeral. Mary Simmonds and Lindy Mahon were at the gate as the two Texans rode up. The girls wore sober black and Mary's eyes were red with tears. But she was controlled and looked relieved to see Dusty and Mark riding toward her. The rest of the mourners were making their way back towards town. Dusty watched Rangoon and the sheriff walking side by side and hoped Hollister did not say anything about the theories they had discussed the previous night.

"Could I have a word with you, please?" Mary asked coming forward. "I'd like to ask you a favour."

"How's Loncey?" Lindy said, before Dusty and Mark could reply.

Dusty swung down from his big paint and Mark dropped from the back of his bloodbay. The big cowhand smiled. "Better. He's too mean and ornery to——"

The words died away before he ended the sentence for Mark did not wish to remind Mary of her father by his flippant reference to his friend.

Lindy and Mary exchanged glances. The small girl seemed to be embarrassed about something. She opened her mouth to speak, then closed it again. Lindy nodded as if encouraging her friend to go on but still Mary did not speak, not straight off. When she began, the words came out hurriedly.

" I saw Mr. Rangoon this morning. He was very kind and understanding when I told him about pappy and the money. I can't meet the note at the bank until the next time our spread's turn comes to sell a herd to the Apache reservation agent."

"Is he pressing for the money?" Dusty asked.

"No, nothing like that. He was kindness itself to me. He's quite willing to give me an extension to tide me over until Tad and Hank are back on their feet. But he says——"

Dusty and Mark waited for the girl to carry on. She stopped, the embarrassment even more plain now. She looked again at Lindy who nodded.

"But what, Mary?" Dusty prompted.

"He wants an older man in charge."

"That's reasonable," drawled Dusty. Rangoon was merely taking a precaution any banker would under the circumstances. It would take a man to run the ranch. "Can't one of the hands take over?"

"We hire a young crew. Not one of them is much over twenty. They're loyal enough to the brand. But there isn't one of them with the experience to run the spread for me. So——"

"You want either Mark or me to handle things for you," finished Dusty as the girl stopped talking again.

Mary's face reddened at the thought of asking a comparative stranger a favour. She knew both the Texans were

93

looking for the men who shot down their friend and might not want to be side-tracked or delayed in their hunt.

"You'll do it, won't you, Dusty?" Lindy pleaded. "It's real important to the Lazy S. Besides—well, you'd better tell them, Mary."

"Mr. Rangoon is sending one of his own men if I can't find anyone suitable."

"Do you know the man he's sending?" Mark asked.

"Yes!" Mary's tones showed she not only knew, but heartily disapproved of the man Rangoon was sending. "I know him. His name's Vance and I don't care for him. Don't ask me why. He's a good enough man with cattle, knows the business. It's just blind feminine dislike. He's big, good looking, a top hand. But he's the sort who gets all cowhands a bad name. Rowdy, stupidly rowdy and wild at times. He drinks too much and acts bad when he's in town."

"That sort of man could stir up a whole of trouble, Dusty," Lindy said echoing Dusty's own thoughts.

"Reckon Rangoon'd accept either of us?" Mark said, his thoughts running parallel to Dusty's.

"Of course. Mr. Rangoon said he would send Vance along only if I couldn't find a suitable man," Mary replied. "Everyone knows you are top hands. The boys would rather ride with you two than with any other men in the west. They hero-worship you." She saw the expression which flickered on the Texans' faces and smiled. "Don't you worry, they won't act that way.

Dusty made his decision. "We'll do it. Mark'll be your foreman, he knows more about the cattle business than I do."

Mark knew that might possibly be true but Dusty's reason for allowing him to be foreman was different. It would leave Dusty free to ride the range and look for further trouble. The foreman's duties would keep him fully occupied with the ranch work and handling of the crew. Dusty did not want to be tied down at the moment for he knew there might be other attempts at making trouble between the nesters and the cattlemen.

"Then we can tell Mr. Rangoon?" said Mary delightedly.

"I'll tell him for you," answered Dusty. "I've got to go and see him."

The girls walked to the town escorted by Dusty and Mark.

At the store, the Lazy S wagon was being loaded by a fat, smiling Mexican. Mark watched his small friend walk on towards the Banking House saloon and wondered what was on Dusty's mind. To the best of his knowledge Dusty did not have any business with the owner of the bank. Shrugging, Mark started to lend the Mexican cook a hand in loading the wagon.

The Banking House saloon was empty of customers as Dusty opened the batwing doors and entered. The games were covered over and two swampers were cleaning the room up. Banjo Edwards lounged at the bar, running a finger down a list on a sheet of paper. The gambler looked up and favoured Dusty with a scowl.

"Your boss in, Mr. Edwards?"

"Sure. In the back. Want to see him?"

"I didn't ask just for the pleasure of talking to you."

Edwards scowled deeper, but he turned and went to a door at the side of the room. He knocked and entered, coming out a couple of minutes after. Dusty spent the time looking over the saloon. It was bigger and more garish than was usual in so small a town. Even with the percentage the gambling tables took, Rangoon would not be showing much profit on the place.

'The boss'll see you," said Edwards as he came out.

Dusty walked across the room, stepping by Edwards, then looking back at him. "This's like it says on the door—private."

For a moment it seemed as if Edwards might object but Rangoon jerked his head and the gambler left. Dusty shut the door and walked towards the big, tidy desk in the centre of the room. Rangoon was busily checking the figures in a book and did not look up immediately. Dusty looked over Rangoon's office. The bank proper lay in a small room beyond the other door. A big, strong-looking safe was in one corner. This and a bookcase were the only other furnishings. Rangoon's guests there being few. The bank's business was carried on in the other room.

The bookcase interested Dusty. The books were mostly on tactics or military history. One book caught Dusty's eye, it was new yet the back was broken. Dusty recognised it and could read the title; Hantley's "Column South. A History of the War Between the States". Dusty was not over surprised to see the book, this was Tom Hantley's home town and Rangoon would buy it show he was proud of the local hero.

"An unusual hobby for a man like me, Captain Fog," remarked Rangoon, looking up with a smile. "Military tactics and history."

"Don't reckon so. Know a man back to home, drinks like a fish, curses worse than a muleskinner and yet he reads Greek classics."

Reaching into his desk drawer Rangoon took out a bottle of blended whisky and a box of cigars, setting them on the desk top before him. "What can I do for you, Captain. Smoke, drink?"

"No thanks," Dusty replied, sitting on one end of the desk. Rangoon set the bottle and box at the other. "I'd like some help from you."

"Certainly, if I can."

"It's like this, Mr. Rangoon. You know why Mark and I stayed on here?"

"Because of what happened to your friend," Rangoon answered. His voice was polite but disinterested, his face mild and bland.

"That's right, because of what happened to the Ysabel Kid. He was wounded, Lindy Mahon made the men think he was dead and they didn't check up. He's still alive, but hurt bad. I've been thinking some about it. The men who are left in that bunch know he can recognise them. They might be back after him."

"The possibility occurred to me, also."

"Now you're a real important man in this section, Mr. Rangoon. Saloon keeper, banker, rancher and all that. Maybe you could get word to the men who hit at Mahon's place," Dusty drawled, waving aside Rangoon's objections before they started. "What I mean is sort of pass the word around that if there's another try at the Kid accidents are going to start happening."

"Accidents?" Rangoon asked. He sat just a little straighter in his chair although his tone and expression did not alter.

"Why sure," agreed Dusty. His left hand Colt came into his hand in an idle appearing gesture. The gun began to spin and revolve on Dusty's triggerfinger, turning like a Catherine wheel. "Accidents. Look at it this way. I can near enough name the man who's behind the raid on Mahon's and the killing of Simmonds. I've not got enough proof to take the man to court, so I'm sitting back and saying nothing. I don't know why he wants to make trouble, this man. All I know is it'd be best for there to be no more tries at the Mahon place. The moment I hear there's been another, accidents start happening."

"What sort of accidents?" Rangoon asked, his eyes on the gun in Dusty's hand. He had often noticed a tendency amongst men who used guns extensively to spin one while they talked idly. It was an exercise which strengthened the trigger-finger. "I'm not sure I follow you."

The four-and-three-quarter-inch barrelled Colt continued to turn and spin on Dusty's finger as if it possessed a mind of its own. "Something real easy. You know how they can happen. Take like now, man fooling with his gun, doesn't mean a thing by it——. Like I said, you own a saloon, could maybe pass the word out for me and pass it strong."

"The word?"

"Keep clear of the Mahon place and the Ysabel Kid. If anything happens to him I'll say to hell with taking time out to get proof—and the accidents start to happen."

The gun stopped spinning at the same moment that Dusty finishing speaking. The bone handle of the Colt slapped into his palm, his thumb eared back the hammer and flame lashed from the barrel of the gun. Rangoon flung back his chair, rising with his right hand flashing up under his coat. The move was fast, far faster than would be expected from a man of Rangoon's build. Then he stood still, hand under his coat. His eyes went to the bottle at the other end of the desk, the cork was shattered by the close-passing bullet.

The door was flung open and Banjo Edwards entered, gun in hand. He stood very still as he saw Dusty's Colt lined on him.

"It's all right, Banjo," said Rangoon without even a tremor in his voice. "Captain Fog was just showing me a trick when the gun went off."

Dusty's lips held a mirthless smile as he watched Edwards holster his gun. The bone-handled Colt in Dusty's left hand whirled once more and flipped back into the holster, then he hitched himself from the edge of the desk. "You'll see what you can do for me, won't you?"

Rangoon pretended to dab sweat from his face. "I'll see what I can do for you, Captain."

Dusty walked across the room, through the door and closed it behind him. He did not even offer to look back and ignored the interested stares of the swampers as he walked out of the saloon.

Rangoon sat down at his desk again. He did not speak for some minutes but when he did his voice sounded harder than usual. The effect was still mild but it did not fool Banjo Edwards.

"Tell the boys to steer clear of the Mahon place from now on."

"But you said——"

Rangoon's hand smashed down on the desk top, the force of the blow made the bottle and cigar-box bounce. "And I just said keep clear."

One thing Banjo Edwards learned early in his association with this mild little man was never to argue with his orders; more so when his voice took on that note of anger. The resulting sound might be amusing—but not to Banjo Edwards; he knew Rangoon too well.

"What happened, boss?" he asked in a worried tone.

"I've just been given a warning; Dusty Fog knows I'm behind the trouble in Gunn River County," answered Rangoon. If he was worried he did not show it. Rather he sounded pleased, as if he welcomed a man of Dusty's calibre suspecting him.

"Can he prove it?"

Rangoon smiled mockingly as he watched the gambler's face. "No. I wouldn't be here now if he could. He's a gentleman, Banjo. Something you'd never understand.

Edwards tried to read something in the bland, mild, gentle looking face; tried and failed. He had seen Rangoon in a tight corner and knew how little fear the small man ever showed. Yet it must be fear which prompted him to alter his plans. Only that morning Rangoon gave an order to get rid of the Ysabel Kid. Now he was cancelling it.

Banjo Edwards' hand shook as he took the bottle and managed to pry out the remains of the cork. He poured himself a drink. Things were not going as they should with his boss. It might be a good time to get out.

Rangoon looked at the bottle and smiled. That was real

shooting. The gun had been pinwheeling around right up until the shot; not much time to take careful aim. The gun just stopped, lined and fired all in a single breath. Few men, and none of them in Rangoon's crew, could have equalled that shot. He laughed as Edwards asked if one of their men could not remove Dusty Fog.

"There isn't a man in the crew who's fit to wipe Dusty Fog's shoes when it comes to using a gun. You'll leave the Mahon place strictly alone."

"You mean give up what you want doing?"

"I don't mean to give up anything at all. I just don't want any added complications. So we leave the Mahon place strictly alone. When the Ysabel Kid's back on his feet they'll be headed to Texas. Send word to the Reservation and tell Juan Jose to meet Jackley out at the line cabin."

"Juan Jose?" Edwards growled. "That damned Apache again?"

"That damned Apache again. Poggy should be here in a few days with the goods I ordered."

"Sure boss," said Edwards. He knew little enough of why Rangoon was stirring up the trouble in Escopeta and did not fancy asking. The small man's plans were made and mostly worked. Only the chance arrival of the Ysabel Kid had spoiled the previous day's scheme, otherwise it would have worked. Edwards studied the other man and took a big chance. "Does Dusty Fog scare you, boss?"

"He scares me. I'm not afraid of the United States Marshal, the sheriff, of Mark Counter or Wes Hardin. They're big men, all of them, but that small Texan is more dangerous than they ever will be. He'd kill me without thinking twice about it if anything happened to his friend. There's loyalty for you, Banjo. Captain Fog would throw over everything, risk being tried for murder, lynched even, to avenge his friend. With that kind of loyalty from my men I could carry out any plan I made."

Edwards scowled. He did not know what to make of the words. What Rangoon planned was not known to any of the men who worked for him. Even Edwards had no more of his confidence. All the gambler knew was he followed orders and received good payment for so doing.

"What're you going to do about them Texans if they don't pull out when the Kid's better?"

"That I haven't decided, Banjo," replied Rangoon thoughtfully. "It's as well not to make any plans when fighting a man as shrewd as Captain Fog. When the time comes we'll strike if we have to. Until then, see the men know to steer clear of the Mahon place."

Dusty left the saloon and headed for the general store. There was no reason that Dusty could see for Rangoon to be causing trouble between the cattlemen and the nesters. He might want land but if that was the case there was plenty to he had for the buying further West. A man so shrewd and smart would not be wasting time stirring up trouble just to get land when it could be obtained cheaper and with less bother . . . There was more than that behind Rangoon's moves. It was something Dusty could not guess at and he did not waste time in trying.

Rangoon was no easy mark, Dusty's every instinct warned him of that. The little man was an opponent worthy of his best tactics. Rangoon was deep, very deep, no fool and far from what his surface appearance made people think he was. The way he had moved when Dusty fired the shot gave warning of that. The move was so fast and practised, Dusty was not sorry Rangoon did not wear a gun. If it ever came to a gunfight Rangoon, despite the town's opinion, would not be a helpless bystander. His draw, had he been armed, was fast, real fast.

Dusty joined the others at the store, Mark put a last sack of flour into the wagon and turned to Dusty with a grin on his face.

"I allus thought the foreman was supposed to tell the others to work, not do it himself."

"You know what they teach an officer, lead by example," answered Dusty. "Is there much more?"

"No, you can come out now."

Dusty turned back to the girls. Mary was unfastening her horse and she looked back, a worried smile on her face.

"Did you see your brother?" Dusty asked.

Mary nodded. She bit her lip as she thought of her brother laying in a bed, only just conscious and not able to speak to her. "I saw him, he couldn't tell me anything, nor could Hank."

Dusty remembered something the Ysabel Kid had told him. "Lindy, the men who hit at your place weren't cowhands, they were hired guns. You might not be able to tell the difference but he could."

"I never thought they were cowhands," Lindy replied.

They mounted their horses and rode from the town, the wagon following them. Mary remembered why Dusty and Mark were coming with her and twisted in her saddle. "Did you see Mr. Rangoon?"

Dusty did not reply for a moment. He smiled, thinking that he had not mentioned the Simmonds ranch. He nodded his head.

"I saw him."

CHAPTER NINE

Mark Counter Takes Over

MARY SIMMONDS brought her mount to a halt, her face drawing into angry lines as she saw what was happening outside the Lazy S bunkhouse. Then she sent the horse leaping forward fast, headed for the bunch of men.

A fight was going on, if fight it could be called, for the two men were not evenly matched. One was handsome, Mark's size, a hefty, rough handful in any company. The other, getting a beating, was a lithe, tow-headed youngster; he was game, but mere gameness could not offset the extra size of the other. The big cowhand laughed and looked at the surrounding circle of faces. The crowd was mostly young cowhands but there were four hard-faced gun-hung men mingled with them.

Slowly the young cowhand forced himself up on to his feet, blood running from the corner of his mouth. Gamely he came at other man. Laughing the big man thrust the wild punch to one side and drove the other fist brutally into the cowhand's stomach folding him over. Up smashed the big man's knee, driving into the cowhand's face and throwing him over backwards. The cowhand lit down flat on his back and the other threw back his head, roaring with laughter.

"Come on, Tommy," he jeered. "Let's see if you can get up."

Mary brought her horse to a sliding halt and dropped from

the saddle, the crowd parting for her to come through. She halted in front of the big man with anger blazing in her eyes.

"Vance, what're you doing here?"

"The boss sent me to ramrod the spread. Tommy here didn't like it. Though I'd show him and the rest of the hands who's boss."

"You keep away from him," snapped Mary as Vance turned back towards Tommy. The young cowhand was trying to force himself up. "Don't you dare touch him!"

Vance laughed, reaching forward to grip Tommy's hair and drag him into a sitting position, then drawing back his fist.

"Let loose!"

The voice was hard, tough and masculine. It brought Vance round to see who had dared to speak to him. His eyes went to the handsome blond giant swinging down from the big bloodbay stallion. Then he glanced at the small Texan who dismounted from the big paint. A grin flickered on Vance's face as the two men came through the bunch of cowhands.

"You wanting something, maybe?"

"Sure," agreed Mark. "I'm wanting to see how you stack up against a man your own size and heft."

"Do huh?" grinned Vance and swung his fist.

Mark Counter moved with a speed and skill which was a joy to watch. His left hand came up, deflecting the punch, and allowing it to pass over his shoulder. The right fist shot out with the full weight of Mark's powerful frame behind it. Vance was not expecting anything like that, he walked forward on to the punch, taking it while off balance. His nose appeared suddenly to burst into agonising pain, his head rocked back and he sat down hard.

There was murder in Vance's eyes as he came to his feet. He rubbed the blood which gushed from his nose, looking at the red smear on the back of his hand. "Dick, Hen!" Vance snarled. "Hold that other one. Spike keep this bunch back. Me 'n' Jack'll see how good the big man is."

Dusty did not get a chance to move, there was a gunman on each side of him. They grabbed his arms, one on either side, holding him. The man standing next to the two holding Dusty, drew his gun and covered the cowhands. Vance nodded and the other man moved in on Mark Counter. Mark acted fast, he backhanded Vance to one side with a swinging smash that almost lifted the dandy from his feet. The other man leapt in, full on to a left swing which spun him around. Mark followed him up with fast-shooting fists as Vance came to his feet once more.

Mary watched, her eyes frightened for she knew what sort of a man Vance was. The two men were going to cripple Mark between them, she was sure of that. Mary licked her lips, then was about to open her mouth to give an order. She knew the cowhands would obey her and jump in to help Mark, even in the face of the gun. Before she could say a word it was too late.

The two men holding Dusty did not expect much trouble from him. They were gripping his arms and were both bigger and stronger. If he tried to struggle they could handle him. Dusty did not struggle, he stood still and his relaxation threw the men off guard. That was what Dusty waited for. Down in the Rio Hondo country, working as valet, servant and odd job man for Ole Devil Hardin, was a small Oriental, thought to be Chinese but actually Japanese. This small, inoffensive man was well learned in certain Oriental fighting techniques which gave him a decided edge over much bigger men. Only to one man had Tommy Okasi taught his tricks. That man was the smallest male member of the Hardin, Fog and Blaze clan. It gave Dusty Fog an advantage which more than offset his lack of inches.

Suddenly the passive Dusty began to move and took the men holding him by surprise. He hooked his right leg behind the man holding his right arm, then thrust back. The man gave a startled yell as he lost his balance. He released the small Texan's arm and crashed down on to his back. Even as the man was falling Dusty struck again. His free arm shot up, over his shoulder as he moved in front of the second man. Gripping the man's head, Dusty bent slightly and brought him flying over, landing hard on the ground.

Dusty was moving with the same speed which made him known as the fastest gun in Texas. The man covering the cowhands became aware that something was happening but did not take his eyes from the crowd. It was a bad mistake but one he did not get a chance to rectify. Dusty smashed the back of his right hand around, driving the second knuckle into the gunman's face just under the nose. Dusty went for, and hit, his favourite spot when dealing with such an emergency. His knuckle smashed just under the middle of the nose, the philtrum, a collection of nerve centres. He hit hard and even taking the awkwardness of the *uraken,* the back-fist of karate, into consideration the result was spectacular. The gunman's head snapped back as if a mule had kicked it. There was a brief look of concentrated and unbearable agony on the man's face as he went down in a limp heap.

Vance and his other man had troubles of their own. They were tough, strong and rough, but Mark Counter was tougher, stronger, rougher and more skilled. Mark's fists shot out, not wildly, but aimed with the skill of long practice. Vance caught a right which spun him round; the other man hit Mark, crashing a fist into the side of his head. Mark staggered and felt Vance catch his arms from the rear. He held Mark while the other gunman smashed a blow into the Texan's face, rocking his head back. Mark brought up both feet and drove them out, the man caught them and reeled back. He snarled, drew his Colt and lunged forward jerking up the gun to slash Mark with the foresight. The man felt a tap on his shoulder and turned to discover who gave it.

Dusty was behind the gunman, the small Texan's right fist coming up as the man turned. The big gunman was lifted on to his toes by the power of the punch, and reeled backwards with arms flailing as he tried to keep his balance.

Mark used all his strength, he twisted and heaved, and Vance lost his hold. Coming around in a tight turn Mark gripped the front of Vance's shirt and pulled. Vance was thrown forward, just missing the man Dusty hit. Mark spun round, interlaced his fingers and smashed them behind the man's neck, knocking him flat on to his face. Dusty caught the staggering Vance with a punch, the man looked as if he was trying to go two ways at once, his feet coming forward while his head and shoulders went backwards. His big body smashed to the ground.

"Dusty!" Mary screamed a warning.

Spinning round Dusty saw that the two men he had thrown were over their surprise and about to enter the game. They were sitting up with hands reaching hipwards in a manner which suggested only one thing. His hands crossed in a sight-defying flicker, the matched guns sliding clear of leather, blued barrels glinting dully as they lined.

105

"Just try it!"

The men sat still; both knew they had called the play wrong. Here was no dressed-up kid trying to appear tough. This was the real thing, one of the fast guns and more deadly dangerous than any they had even seen. They kept their hands clear of guns, for such speed was rarely attained without the corresponding ability to place the bullets where they would do the most good.

Vance rolled on to his face, moving slowly like he suddenly felt old and worn out. He forced himself on to his hands and knees. The young cowhand, Vance's victim, was trying to get up. He looked dazedly at the big man, braced himself and with all his strength swung a punch. Vance was groggy and in no shape to handle a crippled midget right at the moment. He took the punch, it snapped his head to one side and he went down again. His big hands dug into the hoof-churned earth in a convulsive movement, then he went limp. The young cowhand had put all he had got in that one punch and fell forward across Vance.

There was a momentary silence, then one of the cowhands gave a whoop of delight and the others moved forward. Mary and Lindy stood staring at the three unconscious men, hardly able to believe their eyes. Neither girl could see how so small a man as Dusty could pack such a powerful punch. Mary knew of Dusty's skill at cowhand work or with a gun but this was the first time she had ever known he could handle his fists.

Dusty walked forward and looked down at the two scared gunmen. "All right, on your feet, both of you."

The men scrambled up fast. One of them licked his lips and said, "We was only funning, mister."

"Why sure," Dusty drawled and holstered his guns. "I like a good laugh."

His right fist smashed into the jaw of one man, and in the same move lashed the fist backhanded into the other's face. The men rocked under the impact but neither of them made a move to defend themselves or fight back. They knew Dusty and Mark could take them in any kind of fight and did not mean to carry the incident any further.

"Get some water from the well and douse those three," said Mark, grinning. The big Texan knew he had been lucky in the fight. Vance and his pard were rough and hard but they were not skilled fighters. Vance's reputation must have been gained the easy way, against smaller and less able men. Mark looked at the girl, "What would you want doing with them?"

"Get them off the spread," snapped Mary, her face still hot and angry. "I'll tell Mr. Rangoon about this. What started Vance picking on Tommy?"

"Ole Vance come in with the other four," a delighted-looking cowhand explained. "Allowed we ought to head into town and take on some coffin-varnish, then go teach the nesters a lesson. Tommy wouldn't have it, said we should oughta wait here for you. So Vance started into him. Say, friend, how the hell did you hit that feller there. I've never seed a man go down like you done."

The last words were directed to Dusty. Mark Counter grinned, in all the time he had known Dusty, he never managed to work out how the deadly karate and ju jitsu tactics were done. All he knew was they worked and the result was mostly effective and very spectacular. The question remained unanswered for Dusty was busy herding the two gunmen along, getting water to douse the groaning victims of the fight.

Vance was first to recover, he sat up, cursing, as cold water drenched him. The man shook his head, then forced himself to his feet. For a moment he stood glaring at Dusty and Mark, then his hand went to his side. One of the two men caught his wrist, stopping him drawing the gun.

"Don't do it, Vance," warned the man. "I recognise him now, he's Dusty Fog."

Vance's hand came clear of his gun butt, his eyes going to Mary as he wiped the blood from his nostrils. "The boss ain't going to like this. He sent me over to take on as foreman——"

"Mr. Rangoon said you'd take over if I couldn't get a good man," Mary corrected grimly. "I've got two. Mark Counter's acting as my foreman until Hank's on his feet again and Captain Fog's riding for me."

Talk welled up from the group of ten cowhands. They knew Vance to be a top hand but they also knew he was a bunkhouse bully. They did not relish the idea of Vance being foreman, even for a few weeks. None of them objected to the idea of Mark Counter taking on as segundo of the ranch, or of Dusty riding with them. It would be something to boast of, having ridden with the two Texans. There was no objection to Mary's words.

Two of the hands helped Tommy to his feet and to the bunkhouse. Vance stood staring at Dusty, then at Mark, cursing himself for a fool. He had thought the two were just dressed-up kids and knew he had made a bad mistake. If he had noticed the true worth of the Texans he would have acted in a far different manner. He gripped the saddlehorn of the horse one of his men brought him, hooked a foot in the stirrup iron and swung into the saddle. The other two were now on their feet and also mounting their horses, hunched in the saddles and swaying. Vance's eyes were filled with hate as he looked the two Texans over once more.

"I won't be forgetting this," he snarled.

"Get down and make another try, happen that's how you feel," challenged Mark but Vance did not take him up.

Turning his horse Vance rode off across the range, the other four men following him. Mary watched him go and did not speak until the five riders were just dots on the horizon. Her relief was evident for she knew that trouble was narrowly averted and her suspicions correct. Vance would have taken the Lazy S crew into town and stirred up a whole lot of trouble. It was surprising that a mild little man like Mr. Rangoon would hire a bully like Vance and toughs such as the other four. Then Mary thought of the other men at the Flying Fish, they were all of the same kind, not a really good cowhand amongst them. For the first time she was suspicious, then as Lindy spoke to her, shook off the suspicions. An inoffensive, mild little man like Rangoon could not have planned the terrible things which were happening in Gun River County.

"What now?" Lindy asked.

"We'll get settled in at the hawgpen," answered Dusty. "Unless the segundo wants us out and working."

Mark remembered times when Dusty took command, there was rarely any loafing around done then. "Wouldn't be a bad idea at all. We'll take a ride out and look the range over tomorrow. Didn't see much of it as we came in. You'd best take one side and I'll handle the other, Dusty."

"Why sure," agreed Dusty. "Who borders you, Mary?"

The river on two sides. Blayne's on the east and Flying Fish to the right."

"You take the river and Blayne's side, Mark," Dusty suggested. "I'll take the Flying Fish range."

Mark watched Dusty. He knew his friend better than any other living man and he knew something was bothering him. Mark suddenly felt suspicious. That visit to the saloon was for more reason than just asking if they could come to the ranch. Then Mark had a flash of intuition. It was wild, unimaginable, almost beyond any belief; the small owner of the Banking House saloon could not be the one behind the trouble. It was then Mark recalled what Dusty had told the sheriff when Hollister mentioned Rangoon's lack of inches. Dusty was a small man, no taller than Rangoon, yet he controlled and ordered men taller than himself. No, it was a foolish idea. There was only one Dusty Fog, he was a class of man on his own. When they made Dusty they threw the mould away.

"You going to stand there all day, Mark?" Dusty asked, cutting in on Mark's thoughts. "Let's get the gear into the bunkhouse."

The following morning Mark and the young cowhand who had fought with Vance rode the range together. Mark picked Tommy out as the best of the crew, the one most likely to make a top hand. They rode together at an easy pace, making a careful check of everything they saw. Mark knew every facet of the business and knew a well-cared-for ranch when he saw one. The Lazy S crew might be young but they knew their work.

In the late afternoon Mark and Tommy rode towards one of the line cabins the two ranch crews maintained. These were small log huts on the ranch line, one-room buildings with a small corral out back and a lean-to. They were used by members of the ranch crew who were on the far ranges and did not wish to head back to the ranch at the end of a day's work.

The line cabin they were making for lay in a wood. Tommy stopped his horse, looking ahead. Smoke rose from above the tree, a slender plume, not enough to give him any cause for alarm.

"Visitors, probably one of Colt's hands."

"Likely," agreed Mark. "I reckon we'd best Injun up and take a look, what with the way things are."

They left their horses tied out of sight and moved forward

109

carefully. They reached the edge of the trees and flattened down out of sight of the cabin. Six horses were secured outside the buildings, three with saddles, the other three with blankets tossed over their backs. .

"Apache hosses," Tommy whispered. "What the hell are they doing here?"

"Them as waits mostly learns, boy," replied Mark.

Time dragged by, the two men remained where they were. There could be some quite innocent reason for the party being at the line cabin but Mark was not willing to chance it. The way things were in Gunn River County a man did not want to take chances.

The door of the cabin opened and men came out. The first three were squat built, dark-skinned Apache braves. The three who followed them wore range clothes, although one of them was a dark-faced lank-haired man showing more than a little Apache blood. It was this man who was doing the talking, waving his hands in the direction of the range and the town. The three Apaches stood by and all began to talk at once, then stopped and allowed one of their number to carry on. The half-breed listened to what was said and made a reply, looking back at the two white men as if for corroboration.

At the distance they were separated from the house, Mark and Tommy could not hear a word which was being said. There was not a chance of their getting nearer and no use if they did, for neither spoke the Apache tongue. Tommy was looking at the two white men and began to move restlessly. The men wore cowhands clothes, one was a big, hulking shape, the other smaller, both wore their guns tied down.

"Don't work for us or Colt Blayne, none of them," growled Tommy and tensed ready to get up.

"Hold down, boy!" Mark hissed, gripping Tommy's arm with fingers of steel. It was regarded as a serious crime for strangers to use a line cabin except as a place to stay overnight. If the men did not belong to either of the ranches which owned the cabin they should not be there. They most certainly should not be meeting and entertaining Apaches in the cabin.

Tommy was held down by Mark's hand, and made no try to get up. He knew Mark was fully aware of the seriousness of the visit, he also knew it was not fear of a fight making

110

Mark stay down. So Tommy lay by him waiting and watching.

The group at the cabin door was splitting up now, the Apaches mounting their horses and heading off in the direction of the reservation. The three men watched them ride off, then the big one nodded and the half breed mounted his horse.

"Headed for town from the looks of it," Tommy whispered. "We letting him go, Mark?"

"Why sure. Back off and get the horses. We'll ride up like we'd just come to the cabin," Mark replied. "You keep mum and don't let on what we've seen. Not until we get in close and find out what's happening."

Backing off, the two cowhands went to their horses and mounted. Tommy was bubbling with excitement and unasked questions, wondering what Mark aimed to do. It was rare that this line cabin was used for the range here was not the best for cattle. The two men could have bunked down for any length of time without the danger of discovery.

The men turned as they heard horses approaching, the bigger one loosening his gun. For all that, he sounded amiable as the two rode towards him. "Howdy, you ride for the Lazy S?"

"Why sure, this's our line cabin," Mark replied. "Ours and Colt Blayne's."

"That's right. We ride for Colt. Got us up here watching in case any of them pesky nesters try to move this way," said the big man, waving his hand towards the other. "That's Denver, I'm Grat."

"Howdy," Mark cut in before Tommy could speak. "I'm Sam, this's Tommy."

"Light down and take something, coffee's on the boil. Which way's you come?"

"Up from the south," Mark replied. "We're out looking for strays."

"See anybody?"

"Not a living soul," lied Mark. "Who'd be out this ways?"

Mark and Tommy swung down from their saddles, left the horses tied to the crude hitching rail, and entered the small one-roomed cabin. The room showed signs of having been lived in for some time. The two bunks were untidy and the place needed some cleaning. Mark was less interested in the state of the building than in the rifle which lay on one of the bunks. It was long, heavy and unmistakably a Sharps. The Texan gave no sign of what he thought; the other men were in the room now, Tommy looking around in some annoyance at the state of the place. Grat and Denver were at the door, watching every move Mark made.

Slowly Mark's eyes dropped to a pile of clothing laying in the corner of the room. Something blue caught his eye and without thinking Mark stepped forward to pull it from the other clothes. It took him a split-second to know what he was holding; a pair of brand-new, dust-covered bib overalls.

"Mark!" Tommy yelled out a warning.

There was no hesitation about the way Mark moved. He knew just what was happening behind him and reacted with the speed of a master. Even as he flung himself to one side, right hand dropping and bringing out his gun, the roar and concussion of the shot filled the room. Mark heard the flat slap of a close-passing bullet, saw chips kick from the rough log wall. He landed, rolling and fanned off three fast shots. Flame licked from the barrel of his Colt, pointing at Grat as the big man started to swing his gun into line once more. Grat was thrown backwards by the impact of the bullets, crashing into Denver and staggering the man. It was an accident which saved Tommy's life for the young cowhand was no gunfighter and not trained to handle such fast-moving action. Denver's gun was out, lining on Tommy but Grat knocked him off balance and the bullet missed.

Still on the ground Mark threw another bullet into Grat, then started to lunge to his feet as Denver decided discretion was better than valour and hurled himself backwards through the door. Denver hurdled the hitchrail and tore the reins of his horse free, vaulting into the saddle and wrenched the horse's head to make it turn. The horse was running as Mark came through the door, gun in hand and ready for trouble. Mark halted and bellowed an order to Denver to rein in but the gunman did not try, he turned, gun slanting at Mark but from the back of a moving horse there was no chance of a hit.

Mark lifted his left arm shoulder high, rested the seven-and-a-half-inch barrel of his Colt on the arm and sighted. With the steady rest and the accuracy of the long barrel, Mark could call his shots with some skill. The gun crashed and Denver arched his back as the lead hit him. He tried to cling to the saddle, then slowly and almost reluctantly slid to the ground.

Gun held ready, Mark went forward with Tommy behind him. The young cowhand was pale now for he had never seen men die in the roaring action of a gunfight before. The sight was not pleasant. Tommy did not ask the questions which were seething inside him. All he wanted to do was go somewhere and be sick. Mark stopped by Denver's side and rolled the man on to his back. He was still alive although he would not be for long.

"You was with the bunch who killed Simmonds, wasn't you?"

Denver's eyes opened, they were glazed with pain and did not recognise Mark. "Apaches — coming — tonight——"

There was a convulsive shudder and the man went limp. Mark shrugged and put the gun back into leather. He looked at Tommy's face and said gently, "Go behind the trees there, boy."

Tommy turned and went fast. He came back a few moments later, face still pale but looking better. "Mark—I —would you—I don't want the other boys to hear about this."

"I'll not say anything, Tommy," promised Mark. "I was took that way the first time I saw a man killed."

"What's it all about, Mark?"

"Those two in there were part of the bunch that killed your boss. I did a fool trick in there. I should have been set to take them. It was seeing those bib overalls that threw me. Thanks for yelling."

Before Tommy could reply they heard rapidly approaching hooves. Mark drew his left-hand Colt and jerked his head. He was pleased to see that Tommy reacted fast even while feeling as badly as he did. The young cowhand went back onto the porch and flattened down while Mark moved to the side of the cabin. A young man Mark remembered seeing in town and a tall, well-made, pretty, dark-haired girl came into sight riding fast.

"It's all right, Mark," Tommy called and came out from the porch. "It's Sam Blayne and Silvie Rand."

The young man halted his horse, looking down at the body, then lifted his eyes to Mark and tried to move his horse so the girl could not see. Sam Blayne's hand dropped

113

to his gun butt, then relaxed slightly when he saw the Lazy S cowhand.

"What's this all about, Tommy?"

"Found two of them using the shack here, Sam," replied Tommy.

"Two?" Sam inquired, looking at the one body.

"Other's inside, tried to kill Mark here."

"Sure," agreed Mark. "Claimed they worked for you."

"Never saw this one in my life," Sam Blayne answered.

"Didn't allow you had, he's one of the bunch who shot Simmonds," Mark said and holstered his gun. "You'd best come and take a look at the other."

Sam swung down from his horse, glancing at the girl as she sat pale and scared. "You wait there, honey. I'll take a look at him, might know him."

Mark and Sam entered the cabin together, leaving Tommy outside with the girl. The big Texan was wondering about Sam Blayne and this nester girl being together. He smiled, a good-looking girl like that would not be short of visiting young men and Sam Blayne would be real slow if he did not make one of the number. He indicated the Sharps rifle on the bunk and showed Sam the bib overalls but Blayne proved that he was well able to use his eyes.

"Was something said about the man who shot Walt Simmonds wearing nester boots, wasn't there?" he asked.

"Why sure," drawled Mark, looking at Grat's feet and wondering where he kept his eyes. The man's boots were low heeled and square toed.

For some reason he could not explain, Mark did not mention seeing the meeting with the Apaches. He told Sam most of the rest of what happened but decided to leave out all reference to the Apaches until he had found time to discuss it with Dusty Fog.

They heard hooves and a voice came to them. "Howdy gal, you're a mite off your home range, ain't you?"

Sam darted to the window although he knew who was speaking. There was a worried look on his face as he turned to Mark. "It's pappy—well, it's time he found out about us."

"Don't your pappy approve of her?"

"Don't approve of nesters. There'll likely be hell on when I tell him."

114

"Then hold it off for a couple of days," snapped Mark. "We've got enough to make him raise hell over, right here."

The two young men came from the cabin to find Silvie attempting to explain her presence without involving Sam. Her father did not approve of her meeting and walking out with any cowhands and she was sure Colt Blayne would not regard her as a suitable person for a daughter-in-law. Nor did Silvie wish to cause trouble between Sam and his father. She did not want to lose Sam either. It was something of a relief to find that Colt Blayne was more interested in the body than in her.

"Howdy, Pappy," greeted Sam, not knowing how he would explain Silvie away. "Mark here just got two of the men who downed Uncle Walt. The other's inside, Sharps rifle, nester boots, bib overalls and all."

"I'd best take a look," growled Blayne and dismounted.

The men went into the cabin and Silvie Rand sat her horse without a move. She thought she should turn her horse and go but knew Colt Blayne would be just as curious about her absence. He might even form an entirely wrong idea of her being here, one which could make trouble for everyone. She saw the men coming out and heard what Blayne was saying.

"One thing's for sure. Boots or no, that man's no nester. I never saw a fodder-forker yet with hands as well kept as that," he said, his eyes went to Silvie and he was about to say something more.

Mark stepped to the girl's side, looking up at her. "Look honey, I can't take you home right now. I'll let Tommy ride back with you and come over to see you tomorrow some time."

Whatever Silvie Rand might lack in schooling she was far from being slow-thinking. She managed a smile at him although she never felt less like smiling. Her voice was a pleasing southern drawl as she replied.

"All right, I'll see you tomorrow, at the same place."

Tommy was about to go to his horse when Colt Blayne spoke. "You busy over to the Lazy S, Tommy?"

"Allus busy, Colt," Tommy replied.

"Can't have you traipsing off, wasting good time then can we?" Blayne went on. There was a glint of something in his frosty eyes. "Sam here ain't got a thing to do. How about taking the gal home, boy?"

"Me pappy?" Sam asked, startled and hardly able to believe his ears.

"Sure, you. Can't have the hands wasting their time and we can't let a real nice young gal like this ride the range without an escort."

Same Blayne tried to sound nonchalant and unconcerned, as if he would rather be working than taking a pretty girl for a ride. "Sure, I'll take her. Come on, Miss Rand, we'd best get moving."

Colt Blayne watched his son and the girl disappear into the woods, then turned back to eye Mark speculatively. The frosty glint was still in his eyes as he said, "Fine looking gal. Make a good wife for some man. One of the Rand gals. Susan Mae ain't it?"

"Sure," Mark agreed for he could not remember what Tommy had said the girl's name was.

"No, Silvie!" Tommy spoke fast, seeing Mark getting all tangled up.

Colt Blayne chuckled, pure amusement showing in his eyes as he looked Mark over from head to foot. "You're Ranse's youngest boy, ain't you?"

"Why sure."

"Huh!" Blayne snorted. "I might be old and near on ready for sitting back and hardwintering,* but I ain't blind nor dumb." He cackled derisively. "And I'd surely hate to think any Counter ever took a gal off a Blayne."

* *Old timers' hobby of discussing the hard winters they had seen.*

116

CHAPTER TEN

New Winchesters, New Wire

DUSTY FOG was riding the other side of the range with a cheerful Lazy S cowhand known as Howler, a Texas boy who left his home to see something of the West. Now Howler was doing something he never thought he would, not even in his wildest day dreams. He was riding with the Lone Star State's favourite son, the Rio Hondo gun wizard, Dusty Fog. Fowler was bursting with pride but he was not acting respectful or admiringly. He rode alongside Dusty, trying to top the windies Dusty spun about hunting or fishing.

It was shortly before noon and they were looking for a straying bull which took off with a string of cows. The hunt was not successful but they were trying and, topping a rise, looked down on to a well-marked trail. A wagon drawn by two horses was moving along the trail, two men sitting on the box. Howler's face showed relief for he was out of tobacco. That would not be so bad but Dusty was also out and Howler was a smoking addict.

"Let's head down and talk some," he suggested.

"Sure," Dusty agreed, starting his horse forward, headed for the wagon. He saw the men watching him, hands dropping to their sides but ignored the move. In a wild land like this a man took elementary precautions. "Howdy gents."

"Howdy," replied the man driving the team. He was a

117

bearded, dirty-looking man of medium size, dressed in fringed buckskin shirt, old cavalry trousers and calf high Apache moccasins. A livid scar started at the left side of his face, up near the hair-line and ran down into the whiskers. There was an expression in his eyes as he looked at Dusty, as if he thought he should know the small Texan. Then his eyes went to the Lazy S roan Dusty was riding.

"Wouldn't have the makings, would you, friend?" Howler asked.

The bearded man dug out a sack of Bull Durham and passed it over. That was part of the code of the range. A man could ask for tobacco and the request was never refused except as a deliberate insult. The other man looked them over and grinned.

"You wouldn't work hereabouts, would you?"

"Why sure," agreed Dusty and took the sack after Howler got his smoke rolled. "Ride for the Lazy S. We're out looking for strays."

Dusty was sure that he should know the bearded man, but his memory would not work. The man was feeling the same way, Dusty was sure, it was only the horse which was fooling him. Dusty was pleased he had decided to rest his big paint and take out a Lazy S remuda horse.

"Town far off?" asked the bearded man.

"Three, four miles at most," replied Howler, not knowing Dusty was worried by the nagging thoughts, trying to recollect where he had seen the bearded man. "You haven't seen a big roan bull and maybe a dozen or so cows?"

"Lost 'em?"

"Sure, that damned fool bull's wuss'n any Apache for roaming off. Trouble is he always comes back but the cows don't."

"It's hell when you get one like that, ain't it?" the second man inquired, for he had worked as a cowhand and knew the curse of a roaming bull. "Don't know which's the worst a bull or an Apache."

Howler made a simple reply, "Bulls don't tote rifles."

Dusty saw a furtive expression cross the face of the two men. He did not know what brought about the change but it was something to do with the innocent words Howler just spoke that made the men show tension. He saw the hands

118

which left the gun butts as they came up moving back again. Yet not by any sign did he let the two men on the wagon know he had noticed any change.

"This's not going to get that old bull found, Howler," said Dusty, his voice even and friendly. "Let's get to looking for him."

Turning his horse Dusty headed back up the slope. Howler raised his hand in a gesture of farewell and followed. The bearded man sat watching them go, his face scowling and troubled. After Dusty and Howler passed out of sight he started the wagon team forward and growled:

"I've seen that short growed runt some place before."

"Totes two guns," the other man answered. "Don't look hardly old enough to. I bet he bought them to show off with. What you reckon he meant about Apaches and rifles?"

"Just making talk. You know what cowhands are, allus talking."

The man seated by the driver looked back over his shoulder at the boxes in the back of the wagon; some were long, rectangular in shape, others were square. One thing they all showed in common, no sign of what they contained. The man knew what the boxes held and was worried by the casual remark.

"Reckon he knows what's in them boxes, Poggy?"

"How the hell could he?" growled the driver. "Rangoon don't talk, or make mistakes. I bet there ain't more than Rangoon knows about what we've got, or what they're for."

"You worked with him afore this?"

"Yes, up in the Black Hills just after the War. Don't you go letting his looks fool you. He's the hardest man I ever came across."

"Wonder what he wants them for?"

"Revolution below the border," Poggy growled in a voice which warned the other man it was a closed subject and the questions died away.

Poggy did not know why Rangoon wanted the goods he was carrying and did not mean to ask questions either. Like he said, he had worked with Rangoon before and was accepting, if not entirely satisfied, with the explanation given for the collecting of his cargo. Rangoon was not the sort of man one argued with, or questioned.

The two men rode on towards Escopeta without talking, both busy with their own thoughts. They came in by the Gunn River Saloon as the batwing doors opened to allow a man to pass through into the street. He paused on the sidewalk looking at the wagon with some interest, then spoke:

"Howdy Poggy!"

The voice brought Poggy's attention to the man, taking in the gambler's dress, the deputy sheriff's badge and the hat pulled forward so as to throw the face into deep shadow. Slowly Poggy dropped his hand to his side, rubbing the butt of his old Army Colt gun.

"You know me?" he asked.

Wes Hardin stepped forward, left hand thrusting back his hat to allow the tanned face to show clear of the shadow.

"Hardin!" Poggy brought out the word in a strangled gasp.

"As ever was," replied Hardin mockingly. "What're you doing here, old friend of my youth?"

Poggy overlooked the fact that such a question was a breech of Western etiquette and a deliberate insult. "Just making an honest living, Wes."

Hardin laughed, a savage cough of laughter which brought Poggy's hand well clear of his gun butt. "Making a living, an *honest* living, is it. What's in the wagon, Poggy?"

Licking his lips nervously Poggy replied, "Supplies for the Banking House Saloon down there."

"Move over!"

There was no arguing with Hardin. Poggy knew it, and so did the man by his side. Poggy crowded up to his companion and allowed Hardin to climb up on the box. Looking inside the wagon Hardin studied the contents. His eyes narrowed and his voice was a suspicious growl as he asked:

"What's in the boxes?"

Glasses, some fancy likker, stuff like that. Long 'uns hold a new gambling set-up," replied Poggy, fighting to hold his voice even. "Got it on my bill of loading here."

Hardin thought of opening one or two of the boxes but before he could make a move to do so saw the sheriff stepping from his office. Hollister raised his arm and called to Hardin, who reluctantly swung from the wagon and looked up at Poggy, his eyes hard and cold.

"You wouldn't be up to your old tricks now, would you?"

"Me, Wes?" yelped Poggy, well simulated innocence in his voice. "Once's enough for me. I've done with that sort of thing now."

Hardin grunted and walked away along the side of the street. Poggy's hand moved gunwards again but sanity returned to him. He held his move uncompleted and started the wagon forward. He knew that if he shot and missed he would never get a second chance. Hardin would see to that. If he shot and hit, his position would not be much better. Hardin wore a law badge which meant he and the sheriff must be friends. Poggy could not hope to get both sheriff and Hardin. He also knew Rangoon would not want any trouble.

"What's Hardin doing here and as a john law?" Poggy's companion asked.

There was no direct reply to the question for seeing Wes Hardin jogged Poggy's memory. "You know who that short-growed cowhand we saw out there was?"

"Naw, why should I?"

"He was Dusty Fog."

"Dusty Fog?" Poggy's companion snorted. "A short-growed runt like that?"

"Short-growed, or tall as a cottonwood tree, that was Dusty Fog," said Poggy, worry in his tones. "When I've delivered this stuff I'm pulling out—fast."

Wes Hardin walked on along the street and joined the sheriff. They strolled along the sidewalk together. Hardin was frowning, thinking of Poggy coming to Escopeta. The man could be telling the truth, making an honest living, but life had made Wes Hardin a suspicious man.

"Sure wished I could spend half my day in bed," greeted Hollister.

"And me. Just been along to see Frank Gunn. He's got him a touch of the grippe and not holding the game tonight. You look a mighty worried man."

"I am," agreed Hollister. "I saw young Johnny Brace today. He's come down through the reservation. Allows there's a whole lot of council smoke going up."

121

"What's he make of it?" Hardin asked, for Johnny Brace knew Apaches.

"Didn't know for sure. Says Juan Jose allowed it was for a wedding but Johnny allows it wasn't no wedding smoke. They were at the war medicine wickiup. You've heard about Juan Jose, he don't like white-eyes one little bit. Give him a few good rifles and he'd paint for war."

Hardin's face darkened in a sudden frown. The last time he had seen Poggy the man was seated on a horse, a rope around his neck and a quirt waiting to send the saddle from under him. It was the intervention of Dusty Fog and Mark Counter which saved Poggy from hanging as a renegade selling arms to the Indians. Before he could mention his suspicions, Hardin was foiled. Hollister announced that he meant to go home, wash and shave. He wanted to ride out to the place where Simmonds was killed to see if he could learn anything more. Promising to meet Hardin at the Banking House Saloon later for a quiet game of poker, Hollister walked away.

Left to himself, Hardin went into the sheriff's office and sat at the desk trying to decide what to do. It must be a coincidence that Poggy was in town and nothing to do with the Apaches. The man might have turned over a new leaf and was really headed for the rear of the Banking House Saloon. Hardin almost decided he would go along and see the boxes unloaded but called it off. He cleaned his guns and then picked up a copy of the Police Gazette and thumbed through it.

The doors of the office opened and a small boy peeped in. He jerked his head back out again, then looked around the corner of the door, clearly meaning to run if Hardin made any hostile move. The Texan's usually grim features relaxed as he beckoned the youngster to come in, thinking perhaps the boy was bringing a message from his folks.

"Come on in, now, boy," drawled Hardin. "Shouldn't you be in school?"

"School's all done for the day," replied the boy, entering and standing first on one leg, then the other. He looked at Hardin's guns with undisguised interest. "You're Wes Hardin, aren't you?"

"Me, boy? They call me Johnson."

"Shucks, that don't mean a lil thing. You're Wes Hardin,

122

the fastest man on the draw. Is it right you've killed seventy-five men?"

"You've got me all mixed up with Wild Bill Hickok, boy," answered Hardin with a grin softening his face, making him look young and friendly. He could guess why the boy had come to the office.

The boy shook his head. "Naw I've not. I heard how you fooled Wild Bill up in Dodge City. I read about it in one of Ned Buntline's books."

"Ned Buntline never told the truth about anything, boy," replied Hardin. "I was never in Dodge City, nor was Wild Bill."

They talked on for a time, Hardin mentioning other fast men, including his cousin, Dusty Fog. Finally Hardin asked, "What'd you come in here for?"

"You know what them folks down at the Banking House was getting off an old wagon, Wes?"

"I'd bet me a quarter it was a box full of glasses or something."

The boy's eyes gleamed in excitement. "Naw. It warn't glasses. They'd got rifles, new Winchesters in them boxes."

"Rifles!" Hardin growled, stiffening in his chair, his face becoming hard once more. "You wouldn't be funning none, would you?"

"No sir, Mr. Hardin," answered the boy. "Cross my heart and hope to die if I wasn't telling the truth."

"How'd you see them?"

"You know that ole cottonwood tree back of the Banking House? Well, I was up there, can see into the yard at the back and into the room. I've seed some of the gals undressing from that old tree. Waal, I was up there when that wagon come and I dassn't get down again. See, that old Banjo Edwards, he's said he'll whale the tar out of the next kid he catches up there. Well, them fellers started to unload the wagon and they dropped a box. It burst open and I saw the rifles."

"That so?" Hardin drawled, his voice and face showing none of the excitement he felt. "Now look here, boy. We're friends, you and me. You reckon you can keep a real secret?"

"Shucks, I wanted to tell the gang."

"Not yet. See, Mr. Rangoon, he's going to outfit a troop of cavalry from the town here but he don't want folks to know yet. You keep quiet about this until I tell you to let the word out."

The boy looked disappointed at the restriction on his passing out the news. "Aw gee, me and the gang——"

"Tell you what I'll do. You keep quiet about it, don't tell nobody, and I'll let you shoot off my guns. And I'll get Cousin Dusty to let you shoot his as well."

The boy stared at Hardin, hardly believing his ears. For a chance to shoot both Wes Hardin and Dusty Fog's guns he would willingly keep any secret. Hardin saw the excited boy out of the room and took up his hat. He stepped out of the office and walked along the street. Turning into the space between two buildings, Hardin walked through and on to the dusty street which ran at the rear of the Military Avenue buildings. He strolled along, acting as he would if he had been on his rounds as deputy. He stopped under the big cottonwood tree behind the saloon, surrounding the saloon's yard. The wagon stood outside the fence; the gate leading into the yard was open.

Entering the yard, Hardin went towards the rear door of the saloon but before he was halfway Banjo Edwards peered out. There was something about the way the gambler looked which made Hardin change his plans. He had been all set to force his way in but right now did not seem to be the time.

"Howdy, Banjo," he greeted. "Thought I saw somebody hanging about in here, so I came to look. Didn't see anybody."

"Must have been one of them damned kids, they're always fooling about back here," Edwards replied, he stood so that only his left hand showed. Hardin was willing to bet the right hand held a gun. "Thanks for looking in."

"That's all right, I get paid for it," Hardin drawled, then nodded to the wagon. "Taking in supplies?"

"Sure. Some fancy likker the boss ordered. Man'd need a real educated tongue to handle them. He reckons the boys'll buy them."

Hardin grunted a noncommital reply, turned and walked away. He knew there was nothing to be gained by trying to force an entry into the building. Edwards would not be the only man there and they would all be armed. Besides if there were rifles in the wagon. Rangoon might have a perfectly good reason for buying them. In fact he probably did have.

124

The youngster might have been making up the story as an excuse to talk with Hardin.

That night Hardin and Hollister went along to the Banking House Saloon and found the other members of the poker game gathered. Frank Gunn was known to have an attack of the grippe at intervals; mostly when he felt that an all-night poker game was not as acceptable as an all-night sleep. The game would be held in the Banking House for there were few other customers, pay day not being for another three days.

In respect of Hardin's superstition the table was at the side of the room and Hardin's seat against the wall. Facing him across the room was the door to Rangoon's private office. Looking at the door Hardin wondered again about the rifles although he did not mention them. Rangoon was in the game and he was a good poker player, keen, shrewd and with a better than fair knowledge of the mathematics of the game. So were the other players. Hardin forgot his worries and concentrated on the game, any inattention could be costly when matched with good players.

For once, Rangoon was not on his best form. He made a couple of mistakes in his betting and calling which he would not otherwise have done. His eyes kept flickering to the office door.

"I'm not staying in long," he said, studying his cards. "I've got some urgent business coming up tonight and I'll have to pull out when my caller comes."

The other players nodded in agreement. It was part of the etiquette of the game to give notice if meaning to quit before the finishing time. At any other time Hardin would have thought nothing of it, except that it showed Rangoon's knowledge of the game. This night it was different and Hardin found himself speculating who the caller might be. He yawned and looked around the table."

"Don't feel much like an all-night game myself. I reckon I've got me a touch of the grippe coming on like ole Frank."

"Let's all call it a night when Rangoon finishes then," Hollister went on. "The wife's raising all hell because I'm stopping out most nights. Anything for a quiet life."

"Sure," agreed Blinky Howard with a grin. "Anyways, I like to see the law out and about good and early in the morning. Makes me feel I'm getting my money's worth as a tax payer."

"In that case you want to let your taxes lapse," growled Hardin.

The others laughed and resumed the game. The play was brisk and high for about an hour, then the office door opened. Hardin was just throwing in his cards and glanced at the opening door. He saw a dark-faced man looking out, nodding to Banjo Edwards who was at the bar. The gambler crossed the room and the dark face pulled back. The open door was clear for a moment and through it Hardin saw a man. A squat-built man wearing an old cavalry coat, breech cloth and calf-high moccasins. A man with a dark brown face framed with long hanging, lank black hair.

Hardin felt the tension hit him. That was an Apache in there. More it was an Apache wearing the red head band of a chief and there was only one chief in this area, Juan Jose, chief of the White Mountain Apaches, a man who hated white-eyes.

Edwards went to the office door and entered, closing it after him and made sure that when he came out again no one could see inside. He crossed the room and whispered to Rangoon. The small man looked at the other players and smiled.

"I'm sorry, boys. This's the last hand for me."

The other players nodded for they had been warned. The hand was played out and Rangoon pushed back his chair, standing up. The other men took their time but Hardin declined an invitation to go to the bar with the players. He left the room and walked along the sidewalk as if making for the jail. Once clear of the Banking House Saloon he made sure he was not followed then cut between two houses and made his way towards the back of the saloon. He saw the shapes of three horses tied out back and walked nearer. One of the horses swung around, snorting nervously, then a second showed signs of nervousness. That was all the warning Hardin wanted, he knew what kind of horses they were and darted to the tree, flattening behind it.

He was only just in time, the rear door of the saloon was opening just as he took cover. Two men showed in the light for an instant. One was the half-breed Hardin saw in the office; the other an Apache Indian, not the one with the chief's head band. They closed the door and came towards the horses, eyes trying to pierce the darkness. The two men advanced on silent feet, each holding a weapon. Behind the tree Hardin drew his twin Colts but he did not cock them for he knew how keen Apaches' ears could be. He stood, waiting for one or both the men to come over towards him. They stopped by the horses, looking around and then satisfied that the animals were not scared, turned and went back to the saloon.

Time dragged by and Hardin waited behind the tree. He was not sure what he should make of all this and knew there was no chance of his getting near enough to hear what was being said in the room. The horses would give warning of his approach and the men in the room would not hesitate to shoot if they found him spying on them. There were more men in the room than he could handle. He knew that Apaches would not deliberately go out of their way to fight in the dark, but if a fight was unavoidable they could handle themselves, so he did not wish to tangle with the two Apaches in the darkness.

Hardin tried to estimate how long he waited under the tree. It must have been over an hour, he thought, when the door opened and the half-breed emerged with the two Apaches. They mounted their horses and rode off. Soon after, Rangoon and Edwards came from the door and headed for the livery-barn. Hardin wished he could get his own horse without attracting attention. He wanted to know why Rangoon had met the Apaches and where the small man was going.

For all that, Hardin could not believe there was any sinister motive behind the meeting. If Edwards alone was involved Hardin would have thought the worst, but not with Rangoon. It could not be anything worse than selling whisky to the Apaches, the boy must have been wrong about the rifles. If he really saw rifles Rangoon could have some perfectly simple and innocent reason for having them.

With that in mind Hardin made his way around the town, doing his tour as a deputy and finally reached the sheriff's office. Hollister was inside the office, filling in the log.

"Don't know why you bother," Hardin drawled as he entered. "There's never a thing to put in it."

"I know. The tax payers like it though. Makes them think

we're earning our pay. You getting scared of losing, pulling out like that?"

"Nope," replied Hardin and decided to try something. "What'd Rangoon be doing, meeting Apaches at this time of night."

"Don't ask me," answered Hollister, his attention on the log and not more than half listening to the other man. Then the meaning of the words hit him and he let the pencil fall to the desk. *"Apaches!"*

"You all want to wake the dead?" asked Hardin sardonically. "I dearly loves a man who can control hisself. There's no wonder your missus wants you to stop playing poker, way you go on." He paused and eyed the other man mockingly. In the time they had known each other a liking and respect had grown between them. "Course, it might not have been Apaches. Could have been Comanches or Sioux, or Cheyennes maybe."

"Comanches, Sioux, Cheyennes, down this way." Hollister snorted. "This's Apache country and you know it. What the hell would Rangoon be doing with Apaches, anyway."

"Don't ask me. Ask him."

Hollister sat studying Hardin's face for a long moment. "You best tell me all about it, Wes."

So Hardin explained, telling everything he knew. Hollister grunted as he sat listening. "The boy was sure about seeing the rifles, that's what got me worried, Brick."

"What's he look like?" Hollister asked and when Hardin described the boy, grinned broadly. "Young Manny Lieben from the sound of it. He can spin more windies than a Texan talking about Texas. He likely made it all up."

"Could be," agreed Hardin. "What're you fixing in to do about it?"

"Nothing much. We don't know for sure there were any rifles, even Poggy don't prove anything. You allow he was nearly lynched for selling arms to the Indians. Most men'd not want that to happen twice, he could have gone straight. I'm not at all sure what we should do."

"Or me," grunted Hardin. "The hell of it is I've never held a badge before. Look, back home in Texas when there's a problem we take it to Ole Devil Hardin and let him handle it."

"Trouble being Ole Devil isn't here."

"Sure, thought about that," Hardin agreed. Cousin Dusty's here. Let's leave it until we've had a chance to talk it over with him."

Hollister nodded. He had formed a very high opinion of Dusty Fog's capabilities and was willing to go along with whatever Dusty wanted. Still Hollister could not think anything bad of the *small,* fat and friendly man who ran the Banking House saloon.

The morning after found the range quiet but it was a quiet which was soon to be broken. Colt Blayne stretched his feet under the table and watched his son's face, guessing what was on Sam's mind. He was about to suggest Sam brought Silvie Rand over for a meal when the door was opened and a gangling cowhand entered.

"Colt! There's trouble. Somebody wired off that water-hole up on the Rands' line. Got barbed wire right round it, I only just stopped some of our stock hanging on to it."

Blayne came to his feet, rage showing on his face for there was nothing a ranch man hated more than wire. "What! Get the crew out, we'll go over there and see about it."

"Hold hard, pappy," Sam Blayne put in. "Wes Hardin passed word about the next man to cause trouble. Let's go into town and see him."

Blayne scowled, he was never a man to accept argument against his orders but for once held his temper. The boy was thinking for himself, that was for sure. He knew that if the hands went to the waterhole there would be trouble. The Rands would not stand back and allow their fence torn down.

"All right. Get the crew and we'll head for town."

Silvie Rand heard the mournful bellows of the family's milk cows and went up the slope which led to the waterhole on the other side of the rim. She stopped and stared down, then dashed forward, chasing the cows away from the wicked spikes of the barbed wire which was strung right round the waterhole. She looked at the new strands and her face paled. Turning she headed back to the house and burst in on her father.

"Let's take to the hills, pappy," growled Lil Hunk, eyeing his old rifle.

Mrs. Rand slammed the bowl of oatmeal down on the table. She was a big, rawboned and yet still handsome woman.

"No you don't. You know what that Wes Hardin said about the folk's caused trouble. You go into town and talk to him. I'll take the young 'uns across to the Mahon place and pick up all the other womenfolks on the way."

Big Hunk Rand grunted his agreement. He picked up his Sharps rifle and nodded to his two eldest sons; the other five children would go with his wife in the old buggy. Mrs. Rand watched the men leave, then took up the heavy shotgun from over the fireplace, broke it and slid in two shells, then told the girls to get ready.

It was the same story wherever a nester and rancher shared a waterhole, the water was inaccessible, barbed wire strung around it. Tempers rose and men reached for weapons. Then the memory of a soft-drawling speech brought an end to open hostility. Wes Hardin made a promise and gave a warning, he was a man who never went back on his word. So the men headed for town, hard-faced well-armed groups of them riding in silence. Nesters passed cowhands, angry glances exchanged but that was all for they knew Wes Hardin was in town and he would be set to handle any trouble. The nesters made for the Banking House Saloon and the cowhands headed to the Gunn River Saloon. There they waited, grouped in their ranch parties, hard-eyed and silent.

Hardin and Hollister stood at the window of the jail and looked out. "Blayne brought his boys in. Larsen's crew arrived, Major File came in. All Rangoon's boys were here at dawn. Most of the nesters come in. I'll tell you, Wes, I'm scared."

"What the hell's wrong. It's not pay day and even if it was the nesters wouldn't be here," Hardin answered worriedly. "Where's Dusty and the Lazy S?"

Hollister was also worried by the small Texan not being in town. Dusty Fog and the Lazy S would be a steadying influence. If there was to be trouble, Dusty Fog and Mark Counter would be worth a regiment of cavalry.

From outside the jail they heard the sound of rapidly approaching hooves. It was only one rider and the two men looked at the door as they heard boot heels thudding on the sidewalk. The door was thrown open and Tommy came in, face flushed but cool enough.

"Dusty and Mark found one of our waterholes wired off

130

this morning. They sent me into town to warn you there might be trouble."

"We've seen it coming, boy," replied Hardin. "What'd Dusty say?"

"Allows to head for the Mahon place first and see what Mr. Mahon's got to say about it. There's a hell of a lot of smoke coming up from the reservation so Dusty's taking Mary and Lindy with him. He and Mark want to know what the Kid makes of the smoke. Dusty says watch the town and don't let anyone start doing anything loco."

"How we going to do that," growled Hollister. "I want to see all the ranchers and the nesters. Reckon you could bring the ranchers to the Banking House Saloon, Wes?"

"I could surely make a try. You go down there and wait for me."

"Can I help?" Tommy asked eagerly. "I'll do what I can."

Crossing the room Hardin took a Winchester from the rack on the wall. He tossed the rifle to Tommy. "Get some shells out of the drawer there. But don't you start shooting unless I tell you."

Tommy opened the drawer and lifted a box of bullets out, he forced a full sixteen load into the magazine then followed Hardin out and along the street. They entered the Gunn River Saloon and the silence hit them. It was an ominous sign to anyone who knew cowhands. They were a rowdy bunch most times, when in town. If a cowhand was not rowdy it meant there was trouble in the air. All eyes went to Hardin and Tommy as they entered but no one offered to speak. The cowhands were waiting for the bosses to give a lead and the ranchers waiting for Colt Blayne to act as spokesman for them.

At last Blayne spoke, his voice an angry growl. "They've started to wire off the range now. *Our* land, and *they* started to put wire on it."

"Who have?" Hardin's voice was soft and caressing.

"The nesters. Who else? Damn it, Wes, if my crew hadn't found that waterhole we'd have been getting cattle ripped to pieces on the wire."

The crowd rumbled out their angry agreement. It was like the snarl of a lynch mob, a menacing sound. Another rancher got to his feet, a big blond man; his voice, the accent of a Swede deepened by his anger.

131

"By gar, they ban all down in the other saloon right now. All of them no-good nesters. If they want trouble they can have it."

A cowhand yelled his agreement and came to his feet, reaching for his hat. Other men began getting up. Even as he took action, Hardin saw Rangoon with his ranch crew at the side of the room.

"Sit fast, one and all!" Hardin's words were backed by the double click as his matched Colts left leather. By his side Tommy brought the rifle up, holding it hip high and lined, his face set and determined. "Colt, the sheriff wants to see you and the other ranchers down at the Gunn River."

"Sure, and walk right into a trap," Vance, by Rangoon's side, yelled.

"All right," said Hardin, shrugging his shoulders without affecting the way his guns were lined. "I'll go get Mahon and Rand to come along here. Happen *they* aren't scared to take a chance."

The ranchers exchanged glances. The biting scorn in the words hit directly at them as Hardin knew it would. Not one of the ranchers would sit back and allow the Texan to fetch the head of the nesters to the saloon. Blayne got to his feet and looked at his crew.

"You bunch stop here. Sam, you and Johnny make sure none of them come out of here until we get back."

"You boys stay here—understand?" another rancher went on.

His men understood, although they did not like the idea of their boss going into the saloon full of nesters. The ranchers started towards the door, one of them looked at Rangoon, who was coming along, and smiled:

"Ain't no need for you to come along, Rangoon. We'll handle it for you."

For a brief flicker there was annoyance in Rangoon's face but it changed to his usual mild expression before anyone could see it. "I think I'd better come. I might be a moderating influence on you."

The other ranchers did not object, they walked by Hardin and Tommy, through the doors and into the street. The cowhands settled back, but Vance nodded and a lank haired halfbreed who sat at the rear of the room rose and slipped out of the back door, closing it silently behind him. Every ear was

132

straining to catch some sound which would warn them their bosses were in trouble. If the nesters made any treacherous moves the cowhands intended to take a bloody and savage revenge.

The Gunn River Saloon was no more noisy than the Banking House when Hardin entered followed by the ranchers. Mahon and Rand were seated at a table away from the other men, Hollister with them tilting his chair back on the rear legs and nursing a shotgun. The nesters' leaders looked at the ranchers, then at Hardin and Tommy. Nothing was said, the hostile glances were enough to warn Hardin that he was walking on thin ice and that at any moment now a fire underneath might melt it away.

"Let's make some talk," he drawled.

"Who's here for the Lazy S?" growled Blayne. "Where's Cap'n Fog?"

"Him and Mark were out when the word came in," Tommy answered, following the orders Dusty gave him before leaving the ranch. "I come in as the spread's rep."

Blayne nodded his acceptance although he would have preferred the Rio Hondo gun wizard, Dusty Fog. Tommy was a cool hand, it would do him no harm to accept some responsibility. The boy looked firm and grim enough back in the Gunn River Saloon when his rifle lifted to back up Wes Hardin.

"Now gents," Hollister spoke quietly, yet with authority. "Big Hunk here tells me he's found one of the waterholes he uses wired off. So has near on every other farmer here."

"That's why the ranchers are in town," snapped Blayne. "We been finding the same thing. That waterhole we share with the Rands was wired off all way round."

"Which same'd be right smart, if Rand did it. Stop your stock getting to water," Hardin drawled. "And *his*."

Blayne opened his mouth, then closed it again as the import of the words hit him. "Say, I never thought of it like that, but it's right."

"By gar, Wes, I ban out to see that hole I share with Lake there. It was new wire—" the Swedish rancher put in.

"I ain't rich enough to afford wire of any sort," Lake, the nester, spoke up.

"And I sure ain't," the Swede pointed out.

The other men looked at each other. Rand and Blayne

exchanged looks, both thinking the same thoughts. Before Dusty Fog started them all considering the possibility of some outside influence stirring up trouble between the ranchers and cattlemen, none of them would have taken time to think twice. They would have accepted the evidence at face value and painted for war. Now they were willing to try to talk things out first.

Blayne scowled. "It takes a fair bunch of men to lay all that wire in one night. More than any ranch around here hires."

Hardin's face suddenly darkened in anger. He remembered Rangoon's visitors of the previous night. An Apache would do anything to obtain one of those wonderful sixteen-shooting Winchester rifles. He would raid for it, steal for it, kill for it. He might even help lay wire fences in the darkness of the night to get hold of a Winchester. The Texan moved forward ready to say what he suspected.

A glint of something metallic caught Hardin's eye as he stepped forward. It was only a quick glance but Hardin knew what it was and acted with the speed which had kept him alive since being turned outlaw. He came around, hands crossing and the matched guns leaping out. The lead slashed into the bat-wing doors just in time. The hand holding a revolver jerked back, but the shot crashed out. Hardin flung himself across the room and out of the saloon, he heard rapidly-fading footsteps outside. Before he could go and see if there was a chance of catching the shooter it was too late.

Cowhands poured from the Banking House Saloon. They came fast, and with their guns in their hands ready to avenge the treacherous attack on their bosses.

CHAPTER ELEVEN

Apache Rampage

SMOKE ROSE into the air in a thickening black cloud. Dusty Fog and Mark Counter halted their horses and the two girls stopped behind them. Dusty sent his horse up a slope and looked down the other side. He heard the others following and was about to stop them. Mary brought her horse to a stop by his side and gulped. Lindy gave a gasp and turned her head away from the sight below. A wagon was burning at the foot of the slope, two shapes laying by it, stiffening on the ground. Dusty told Mark to take the girls back out of sight and rode forward.

It was not a pretty sight. The two bodies were mutilated but there was enough of them for him to make an identification. He looked down at the pain-wracked and agony-twisted features of Poggy, the renegade who sold arms to Indians. Dusty still could not remember who the man was. The hole between Poggy's eyes meant nothing more than he had been shot. His empty holster and the clean stripped loops of his belt told their story as did the mutilation. The Apache never took scalps preferring more basic trophies.

Turning his horse Dusty headed back to the others. Mary looked at the cold, grim set of his face and felt a shudder run through her. Never had she seen Dusty look so disturbed.

"What was it?" Lindy gasped. "An accident?"

"Nope. Start those hosses for your place as fast as you can. The Apaches are out and they've got rifles," answered Dusty. "*Rifles*—!" Memory flooded back to him of a man sat on the back of a horse with a rope tied around his neck and a cottonwood tree spreading its great branches overhead. "Poggy. Now I remember him. Poggy, the renegade. Lord, Rangoon wouldn't try a thing like that."

"Like what?" Mary asked. Mark did not need to for he remembered Poggy.

"Come on, put those petmakers to work!"

The very urgency of Dusty's voice ended Mary's questions. Obediently she used her spurs to make her horse move faster. Lindy followed her friend, worried by Dusty's attitude and puzzled by his words. She watched the way Dusty and Mark were acting and felt fear creeping over her.

Dusty reached down and drew the Winchester carbine from the saddleboot. For once in his life, although he would never admit it to Mark, he wished he was carrying a rifle, with the full sixteen-shot magazine capacity instead of the twelve his carbine supplied. The loads in the carbine were all he brought with him for he had never expected anything like this. He also wished he was riding his big paint instead of one of the Lazy S rough string. The paint was an animal he knew he could rely on and trust when under fire, he did not know if this horse would allow him to use weapons from its back. Mark was also riding a Lazy S horse, a big brown stud which ate work and would carry his giant frame. He was nursing his rifle as he rode and Dusty guessed Mark was wishing he had got more than the bare loads for it.

They held the horses to a fast trot over the rolling folds of the range. All the time Dusty and Mark were keenly alert and watchful but they saw no sign of the Apaches. The range looked empty of life but the distant smoke from the reservation was now going. That was a bad sign, it meant the council was over, the fires dying out and the braves riding.

"Hold it!" Dusty said, bringing the others to a halt as they topped a rise. "What do you make of that, Mark?"

In the valley below them, winding along in an untidy straggle were several buggies, each driven by a woman and most of them with children in the back. Apart from a few boys in their early teens there was no sign of men in the party.

"They're our people," Lindy gasped out. "Almost every family in the valley and it looks as if they're headed for my home."

"Let's go talk to them, then!" Dusty ordered.

Mark suddenly jerked his head without speaking. It was a sign Dusty caught even though the girls did not notice it. Following the direction of Mark's gaze. Dusty saw a cloud of dust, the faint shapes of riders under it. He did not need to look twice to know what the riders were. Nor to guess that the riders had seen them and were headed their way. He started his horse down the slope, following the girls.

Mrs. Rand watched the approaching riders with grim eyes, she gripped the butt of her shotgun even though she recognised Lindy. Her eyes missed nothing, catching the smile on Silvie's face as the girl recognised Mark.

"Howdy ladies," greeted Dusty, raising his hat. "Going for a picnic?"

"What if we are?" growled Mrs. Rand, hefting the shotgun.

"Like to ride along with you, ma'am, happen you are," answered Mark. "We don't know the range hereabouts and might get lost."

"Get lost, huh!" Mrs. Randy grunted, her eyes going to Silvie again, then to Lindy and Mary. "You stand a good chance of getting lost with those two gals."

"Start the wagons, ma'am," Dusty's drawl was firm and grim. "There's Apaches on the warpath and they're coming fast."

Dusty guessed the woman's type right, she would not panic at the word, "Apaches." Without even batting an eye Mrs. Rand nodded to Silvie and the girl started her team forward. The other buggies moved slowly along, but Mrs. Rand pulled to one side to allow them all to pass her. Her eyes were on Dusty and Mark, wondering if she could trust them. They were cowhands, and at the best of times the cowhand was a practical joker Yet she did not think there was any joke this time. That small Texan's face was too grim and set for a joking matter. Apart from the odd shotgun the women were not armed, her own girls could all use weapons but they did not have any with them. If Apaches came on them out in the open they would be in a bad way.

Dusty was just as aware of their state in the event of an

attack. They would have no chance at all unless they could reach the Mahon place and fort up. With this in mind he started to give his orders.

"Mary, tell Mark the best way to reach town from here. Mark, you-all cut aross the range and get help for us. Most of the ranchers'll likely be in town over this wire trouble. Lindy, when Mary's finished you and her get on ahead. Tell your mammy to get out all the ammunition she can lay hands on and keep the front door open ready. We'll be coming in fast when we arrive."

There was no arguing or discussing Dusty's right to give orders. Mark knew Dusty was the best man to run the defence of the house and that his own chore was by far the safer. He listened to Mary's range geography lesson, then headed his horse in the direction she gave him. Mary and Lindy did not waste any more time, they put their petmakers to use and sent their horses racing off, headed for Lindy's home.

Dusty rode up the slope and looked over the range, the dust cloud was close now; too close for comfort. He could make out the individual Apaches and see the rifles they held in their hands, new Winchesters. Even as he turned his horse Dusty could guess what happened and swore he would get Rangoon for arming the Indians. Right now there was not the time to waste, flight was the only hope for the women below. He raced his horse down the slope and Mrs. Rand caught his signal, reached down for her buggy whip and ordered her family to hold tight.

"Apaches coming, move out!" Dusty roared. "Yeeah!"

It was the rebel war yell, a cry many a Yankee army man had learned to hate in the Civil War. Dusty screamed it out as he caught alongside the first wagon and jerked his boot from the stirrup iron to kick the horse in the ribs. The old buggy horse, a cull from some ranch remuda, still retained enough fire to take exception to such treatment. It lunged, slamming into the harness and hurling the buggy forward. The woman driving it was middle-aged and looked as if she knew what to do, she did not panic and held her horse under control. Behind her the other women were all urging their horses on. Everything now depended on the distance to the Mahon house, how far behind the Apaches were—and the driving skill of the women.

Dusty brought his horse to a halt, allowing the buggies to go by him. He was wishing he had taken Mark's rifle to augment the arms of the party but it was too late. Mark was a dot on the horizon and there was no chance of getting him back to collect the weapon from him. So Dusty rode at the rear of the party, ready to go forward and prevent any buggy leaving the track they were following. The track was not ideal for fast driving but it was safer than the range; once a buggy left the track there was every chance it would break an axle or overturn.

From behind came the deep drumming of fast-moving hooves and the wild yells of the Apaches as they followed. It was a sound which was guaranteed to scare anyone who had ever heard it before and made the women lay their whips to the racing horses.

Dusty sent his horse hurtling along the racing line, crowding a scared woman's buggy back into line. "Don't try and pass!" he yelled. "Keep in line."

The warning was taken and the women held their racing horses to the track, no more attempts at overtaking were tried. Behind, the Apaches were closing the gap with every stride of their war ponies; it would be a close thing. The Mahon place was ahead but the Apaches were coming up fast and the women would have to get into the house. Dusty saw Lindy, Mary and Mrs. Mahon come out of the house and look in the direction of the buggies. The woman gave an order and the two girls went back into the house but she stayed outside holding the new Winchester in her hands.

The first buggy was slowing by the gate now, the woman and her child getting out. She yelled and the horse started forward, pulling the buggy out of the way of the next to stop. This was the most dangerous time. The buggies stopped and allowed the families to tumble out and run for the house. The yells of the Apaches were growing louder all the time, scaring the women. The Rand family would be the last to unload but they were also the coolest.

Dusty brought his horse around in a turn, started to lift the carbine and remembered just in time he was not on his paint. He came down from the saddle and lifted the short carbine, sighting it. The Apaches were urging their horses on at full speed, each brave wanting to be the first to count coup on the white-eye women.

139

Dusty sighted carefully, he did not have more than twelve shots for his carbine and must make every one count. The Winchester carbine was a short-ranged weapon and not too reliable for shooting at over seventy-five yards. The Apaches were within that range now. He fired and saw a brave go backwards over the rump of his racing war pony. From Dusty's side came the hoarse bellow of a shotgun and a second wild racing, war-yelling brave left his horse.

Without taking his eyes from along the barrel of the carbine Dusty asked, "They all in the house yet, ma'am?"

"Just about," Mrs. Rand answered, cocking back the hammer for the second barrel of her shotgun.

"Move back then, ma'am. Run for it."

The shotgun coughed again and the nearest brave was knocked flying from his pony. Dusty heard Mrs. Rand running across the garden and his carbine spat twice. Dusty might often say he was no hand with a long gun, but when the chips were down he could take pointers on markmanship from no man, up to and including the Ysabel Kid. His two shots were meat-in-the-pot hits, one brave was down, a second's horse rolling in the dirt.

"Run for it, mister!"

Dusty heard Mrs. Rand's yell and turned. It seemed that every time he came to the Mahon place he ended up running across the garden, making for the door. The Apaches were shooting now, seeing there was no chance of counting coup on the small white-eye. However from the back of a racing war-pony and with a weapon new to their hands none of the braves made a hit. Dusty hurled himself the last few feet, through the open door and into the house. Mrs. Rand showed she knew what to do in such a situation, she slammed the door behind the small Texan and slapped the locking bar into place.

Dusty was about to make for the living room and organise the defence of the house when he heard voices raised in argument from the Kid's bedroom. Dusty went along the passage fast for he knew what to expect. In spite of the danger a grin came to his face at the sight.

The Ysabel Kid was on his feet, swaying and trying to shove by Mary and Lindy. It was a good thing neither of them spoke much Spanish for some of the things he was saying to them would have made their hair curl.

140

"Let go of me! Damn it all to hell!" the Kid roared when Spanish curses got no results. His face was pale and lined with agony caused just by being on his feet.

"Lon!" Lindy gasped. "Get back in your bed. Stop it! You'll open the wounds!"

"All right, Lon!" snapped Dusty. "Get back in that bed."

"Like hell!" growled the Kid. From outside they could hear the yells as the Apaches circled the house before attacking, and the bark of weapons. "I'm going——"

"You're back in bed, or I'll put you there," Dusty warned, then he saw a way to make the Kid behave. He studied the night-shirt his friend was wearing, it belonged to Mahon and was considerably more elegant than anything the Kid's usual attire. "Get back in bed, you'll be more use there than laying on the floor. Man, I'd bet ole Red, Doc and Waco'll have a laugh when I tell 'em about that fancy night-shirt you're wearing. They'll surely all want to buy one."

The Kid instantly became contrite and obedient. He allowed himself to be lowered on the bed and lay back. The effort at getting up had sapped most of his strength but he knew he must try and help. His eyes went to Dusty and he growled, "You tell the boys about me and I'll fix your wagon, but good."

Dusty laughed. The other members of the floating outfit would never know of the Kid's fancy taste in night-wear, but it was a good way to keep him in line for the future and Dusty stowed the thought away. He picked up the Kid's gunbelt and laid it on the bed then turned to Lindy.

"Open the Kid's warbag and get his other gun out, you'll likely need it. Mary, go in the dining-room and see if you can get a weapon."

Lindy opened the warbag and withdrew the Kid's second Colt Dragoon. It was not a pair with the gun in his holster, but one of the round triggerguard, Third Model, butt cut for the attachable stock. Lindy lifted the canteen stock out and could not help but look at the plate in the butt. She read he inscription and wondered how such a fine weapon came to be in the Kid's hands for he definitely was not either of the men named on the plate.* She looked at the weapon, not knowing much about guns and not sure if she could handle

* *The answer is given in TRAIL BOSS.*

141

such a heavy revolver. The Colt Dragoon was percussion fired and she knew how to load it but nothing more.

"Slap that butt on, gal," drawled the Kid. "She's full loaded and only needs capping. You'll find the caps in the buckskin bag there, with the pistol balls."

Lindy took out the Kid's powder flask and bullet bag but her hands would hardly obey her as she fitted the caps on the nipples, readying the gun for use. "I'm frightened, Lon," she gasped.

"Sure, gal," the Kid's voice was cool and even, steadying her nerves. "Just you come and sit by me. Watch that window with one eye. You capped her all right so the rest'll be easy." He watched Lindy holding the stock; it was like the butt of a rifle, with extensions at either side, a piece to hook under the bottom of the pistol's butt and a screw on top. "Put those bars there under the shoulders of the frame and the strap under the butt." The girl obeyed, the extensions fitted into place and she looked for her next orders. "Tighten that screw on top. Do it as tight as you can."

Lindy obeyed. It said much for both the ingenuity of the inventor and the workmanship of Colonel Colt's Hartford factory, that the girl found herself with what amounted to a six-shot carbine on her hands. She looked at the gun, then at the Kid. "What now?" she asked.

"Get to that window and bust it. If any of them come at you let them get in so close you can't miss. Don't worry none, she's loaded with forty grains and a soft lead ball. That'll stop a man dead in his tracks; he won't come in nearer if you hit him any place."

Lindy went to the window and looked out. She broke the glass with the butt of the carbine and looked out. The Apaches were circling the house, riding their ponies with skill and grace, shooting as they went. So far they were not attempting to charge the building, but from different rooms came the crack of the few weapons. Dusty's voice reached her ears ordering the women to hold their fire unless they were sure of making a hit. Dusty was worried about their lack of ammunition. It would take Mark some time to get into town and bring help back. They would have to hold the house until relief arrived.

Suddenly four braves hurtled over the fence and came

142

towards the back of the house. Lindy stared at the squat, dark-faced men and was afraid, she had seen two men coming towards her in the same manner and missed them. Lining the Dragoon, Lindy let the hammer fall. The gun bellowed. Due to its heavy powder charge and comparatively light weight it kicked harder than the Springfield. Through the smoke she saw a brave stop in his tracks, foot raised from the ground. Then he pitched over backwards. She gasped, suddenly realising she had killed a human being.

One of the remaining braves fired his rifle; it was held hip high and by sheer chance the bullet smashed through the window grazing Lindy's head, dropping her to the floor. The three braves were at the window, their dark faces leering in. From behind them and on the other sides of the house, another attack was beginning.

Forcing himself up on his pillows the Kid gripped his old Dragoon in both hands. He gave a wild rebel yell and fired. One of the Apaches reeled back, his face burst into a mask of blood. A second brave hurtled at the window and came through in a crashing of glass, landed on his feet and lunged forward. A hand caught his shoulder, turned him and a fist smashed into his face. The Apache was knocked backwards on to the bed, and never got a chance to recover. The Kid let his gun fall on the blankets and whipped up the bowie knife in his left hand. The right hand gripped the Apache's lank black hair, drew the head back and exposed the throat to the great, ripping blade of the bowie knife. Sharper than many a razor, the eleven-and-a-half-inch blade bit down on to the brown throat, sinking in deep, then coming out. For an instant the great cut was clear, then blood spurted from it for the Kid's knife lay in the Apache's throat open almost to the bone.

There was no time for Dusty to get his guns into action, for two more Apaches were in the room. One hurled himself at Dusty, the other drew his knife and flung himself at the Kid. The brave was almost on the Kid, knife lifted for a killing blow. Dropping his knife the Kid lifted the old Dragoon and fired from a range of not more than three feet. He could not miss, but with a lesser weapon, one without the man-stopping power of the old Dragoon, the Kid would also have died. The Apache's momentum would have carried him on to plunge the knife home. As it was, the ball struck the brave and knocked him backwards across the room. The Kid fired at another brave who came to the window and the Apache drew back.

The second brave was hurtling at Dusty. A squat powerful warrior, bigger and heavier than the small Texan. He came with a knife in his hand for it was counted a greater triumph to take coup with a knife than a rifle. He appeared to knock Dusty over but the Texan was going down before the man hit him. Catching the man's dirty shirt Dusty pulled as he went backwards. His shoulders hit the floor but his feet went into the Apache's stomach. Pulling down on the shirt Dusty heaved up with his feet throwing the brave over. It was a well-done trick but the Apache was no mean hand at wrestling. He was taken by surprise but landed with an almost cat-like agility, going through the door and into the passage, still holding his knife.

They both made their feet at the same moment and the Apache came in again, lifting the knife for a stab. Dusty went under the slashing blade. His right hand stabbed out, fingers extended and held together thumb bent over the palm. He used the karate *nukite,* the piercing hand, driving his fingers full into the Apache's solar plexus. The brave gave a strangled cry and doubled over as if he had been kicked by a mule. Dusty struck again, clenching his fist and smashing it with all his strength against the Apache's temple. The warrior was knocked sideways, his head smashed into the wall and he went down in a limp heap.

Dusty wasted no more time on the Apache, he was out of action for a long time, if not permanently. He saw the Kid was still able to shoot and that the window was clear, then heard Mrs. Rand yell and darted from the room.

Lindy was on her hands and knees, she reached up and touched her head, the fingers came away red and she forced herself on to her feet, staggering to the bed. Her foot touched something which yielded and she looked down, then gave a scream. The Kid's knife-killed victim was anything but a pleasant sight. Lindy lost control of her nerves and began to cry hysterically. The Kid's hand slapped hard across the girl's face and her sobs died off: His voice was weak but still held a bite to it.

"Stop it, gal! Quit that yelling, will you! Go get me the other gun and make a start at loading this one."

The Kid knew Lindy's wound was not serious and watched to give the girl something to take her mind off what she had seen. Lindy's eyes went to the bloody sight on the floor but she held herself in control. Picking up the carbine-stocked Dragoon she brought it to the Kid and then with shaking hands started to strip the spent caps from the other gun.

The Apaches rushed at the front of the house, smashing down the fence and churning over the garden. Mrs. Mahon and Mrs. Rand used their guns from the windows, firing at the charging braves. Mrs. Rand centred her shotgun on two braves who were hurtling forward ahead of the others. She fired and saw one go down, the other only caught a couple of balls in the side, they hardly slowed him down. The shotgun coughed again but Mrs. Rand missed the man she aimed at and sent another rolling over in the dirt. She saw her mistake, the brave hurled himself headlong through the window, smashing glass and sash. He grabbed the shotgun as he came in. Mrs. Rand knew she could not hope to hold it so she let go and her hard, bony fist smashed into the Apache's face. It was a good punch and thrown by an arm powered with muscles many a man would have liked to own. The Apache's head snapped to one side and he crashed to the floor. Mrs. Mahon spun around, firing the rifle. Her first shot struck the Apache in the head, rendering any further attention unnecessary.

The window was crowded with Apaches, all trying to get in. Mrs. Rand let out a yell of, "Texas"; and dived for the shotgun. The other women in the room started to yell and scream, getting in each other's way as the Apaches were doing at the window. Every brave wanted to get into the house and at the white-eye women. So they crowded up, and struggled instead of taking their time.

Mrs. Rand caught up her shotgun but she knew there would not be time to put in more loads. Then she saw the shape of a man at the door. A man? A smoke-wrapped devil with a roaring Colt in either hand. Dusty was coming through the door, his matched guns spewing out lead as fast as his ambidextrous prowess allowed. The window was suddenly cleared under the smashing hail of lead, the Apache attack broke and the warriors pulled back outside the fence.

"Get one of the ladies who can handle a gun to go to help Lindy," Dusty ordered as he went to the table and started

145

to reload his Colts. "She took a bullet nick, not bad, but she'll need help."

"You go, Lou," Mrs. Rand said for Mrs. Mahon was very pale. "Let Susan Mae have your rifle and use Lindy's gun."

"I'll go with you, ma'am," drawled Dusty. "I want to hear what Lon's got to say about things."

Mrs. Mahon and Dusty went along the passage and into the Kid's bedroom. The woman stopped and stared at the three dead Apaches. There was horror in her eyes as she turned to Dusty and pointed to the one on the floor, the Kid's victim.

"Did you——?"

"No, ma'am, I just tossed them to ole Lon and he did it."

"Caught me the big 'un myself," growled the Kid. "Get shut, Lindy's telling me what the Apaches are doing."

Lindy was by the window, peering out cautiously. She turned and said, "They all pulled back, left a couple to watch the house and went around the front. Is that good, Loncey?"

"Not good, or bad as it stands on the face of things," replied the Kid, his voice weak but definite. "They've been held off once and they're going to make some medicine. Happen they get the right answer they'll try again. We'll be under them, belly deep and they'll take a powerful heap of stopping."

"Get your head fixed, gal," Dusty ordered. "Anybody hurt yet?"

"They got Mrs. Feisten, wounded a couple more," Mrs. Mahon answered. "We're almost out of bullets."

"Yeah, I know," Dusty said. The situation was serious and the next attack would be forced home with more determination than the last. "Load everything that shoots and get ready."

"But don't let nobody start shooting unless they can hit," warned the Kid.

Mary came in, face smudged and dirty but grim.

"They've killed a horse, got a fire going and are cooking it."

"That means we've got a few minutes, Dusty," the Kid drawled, laying back for he was nearly exhausted. "They'll eat before they come in, but when they come — Lord, they'll come for keeps."

Dusty finished loading both the Kid's Dragoons for him.

146

Then, before he turned to make a round of the house and see what he could do about the defence, Dusty looked at the Kid and nodded to the two women. The Kid caught the sign and gave his affirmative nod; if the Apache got into the house he would make sure neither woman fell alive into their hands.

In the town of Escopeta men poured from the two saloons. The nesters, wanting to know who had tried to use the gun from the door, the cowhands thinking their bosses were in trouble. It was unfortunate that no rancher managed to be amongst the first men out of the Banking House Saloon. The cowhands saw Hardin leave the saloon followed by armed nesters and drew the conclusion that their bosses were in bad trouble. The nesters saw armed cowhands bearing down on them and took the line that they were in danger.

"Hold it, all of you!" Hardin barked out the order to the advancing cowhands.

"Keep going, boys," a Rangoon man shouted from the back of the crowd. "He won't shoot!"

The cowhands hesitated. They knew Hardin's reputation and knew he would not give the order unless he meant to back it with a brace of smoking Colts. In the cowhand bunch Banjo Edwards saw the hesitation and growled an order for one of the Flying Fish men to down the Texan. He knew that if one man started shooting it would spread. Not one man would wait, but would start his gun talking. Wes Hardin was good with his guns but he could not handle the entire crowd. They would get him and the fight become general.

A wild, rebel yell rang out, sounding over the silence before the storm of violence. Loud it rang, and the men heard the rapid beating of hooves as a rider tore towards the town.

"Apaches are out!"

The yell brought a halt to every move. It was the only cry which could have stopped the trouble before it started. When the Apaches were out all white men needed to stand together. Every eye went to the big man who rode into town. The horse staggered as it came towards the cowhands, passing the nesters.

Mark Counter felt the horse give out under him and kicked his feet free of the stirrups. It had run with Mark's great weight and given its all. Mark sprang clear as the horse fell.

147

He staggered and only his iron will kept him on his feet but he faced the crowd. His horse ran to death under him but he had reached the town.

Wes Hardin was by Mark's side, holding the big cowhand erect until he caught his breath again. Frank Gunn, over his grippe, forced through the crowd with a bottle in his hand. Mark took the bottle and drank deeply from it, then looked around at the crowd. Nesters and cowhands mingled together now, waiting to hear what he had to say.

"The Apaches are on the warpath," Mark got the words out as fast as he could manage. "The nester women are at Mahon's place, forted up and Dusty's trying to hold the Apaches off."

There was no thought of feuding now, no hatred. Apaches were threatening womenfolk and the men in the crowd were as one.

"Get your hosses!" Sam Blayne yelled.

"Come on, Big Hunk!" Colt Blayne bellowed. "Young Silvie's in trouble."

"Hold it!" Banjo Edwards snarled the words out, pushing through the crowd. "He's lying, there's——"

Mark thrust Hardin aside. At the same moment his hands dropped towards the butts of the ivory-butted guns. In the West a man did not use the world 'liar' unless he was willing to back it with a roaring gun. Banjo Edwards was also going for his guns, taking his chance to match shots with Mark. He would never have a better opportunity to beat Mark Counter for the big Texan was exhausted from his ride. Even so, Mark's long-barrelled Colts were clear ahead of the gambler's. Flame lashed from the barrels. Edwards was kicked backwards from his feet by the force of the bullets, his own guns just clear of leather, but he died without having time to line them.

The half-breed lunged from the side of a building, his gun slanting up and at the same moment Vance started his draw.

"Vance!" Tommy yelled and brought up the rifle, firing from the hip. He saw the big cowhand jerk back as the bullet hit him. Then the crash of Hardin's guns, as he threw down on the half-breed, shattered the air.

The other Flying Fish men stood still, not knowing what to make of the scene. Only the three who now lay dead were deeply involved in Rangoon's plans. The others were ready to go and help rescue the white women from the Apaches.

Even as the smoke rolled from the street, Mark thrust his guns back into leather. "Get me a horse," he growled.

"Rest up, boy," Blayne answered, gripping Mark's powerful arm. "You've rid far enough and there's enough of us to handle things."

"Like hell!" Mark snapped back. "Dusty and Lon're out there. I'm going with you, to help them."

A Flying Fish man came up leading a big horse. "Here, Texas, take this. It belonged to Banjo but I don't reckon he'll be needing it."

Rangoon stood on the side of the street, watching everything. A half-smile played on his lips. His final plan was spoiled, there would be no chance of his starting again, not with what Dusty Fog suspected. He gripped the sleeve of one of his men.

"Ben, if Captain Fog's still alive tell him I'll be at the Flying Fish, waiting for him."

"Sure boss," replied the man and ran for his horse.

Rangoon watched the men riding out of town. Nesters, cowhands, riding in harmony and for a common purpose. Turning he went back to the bank, opened the safe and took out a carpet bag. He stuffed some of the money into the bag and left the rest locked in the safe. Regretfully he walked from the room, went to the livery barn and collected his horse to ride to his ranch.

The rescuing party reached the Mahon place just as the Apaches launched their big assault. Hitting the braves like raging tornadoes the white men broke the attack and scattered the Indians. Then it was over, the Apaches who could, running for the safety of the reservation and seen on their way by a bunch of cowhands.

There were happy reunions as the nesters went to their women. Silvie Rand flung herself into the arms of Sam Blayne and their fathers stood grinning at each other. Peace was on the land, the leading families of both sides were to be united.

Mark and Dusty came together, neither spoke for a long moment but their handshake told a story. Mark grinned and drawled, "Lon all right?"

"Why sure," answered Dusty. "You get any tobacco while you were in town?"

It was then that the Flying Fish cowhand came up and delivered Rangoon's message. Wes Hardin loomed up, face hard and grim. "Dusty, Rangoon——"

"I know, Wes," replied Dusty. "I've known all along. Get me a horse."

Colt Blayne loaned Dusty his big horse without asking questions, even when Dusty ordered that the Flying Fish men should be held under guard until he returned.

"Do you need any help, Dusty?" asked Mark, watching his friend mount the horse.

"No, I'll handle it. You take care of things here."

The Flying Fish men were rounded up, disarmed by Mark and Wes Hardin. One of the men growled, "What the hell, Wes?"

"You'll know when Dusty gets back," Hardin answered. "Keep them here, Colt. I want to go in and see the Kid."

"What's this all about, Wes?" Hollister asked, coming up from behind the back of the house. "These're Rangoon's men."

"That's sure enough true," Hardin answered. He smiled mockingly at the men who stood looking at him. "And Rangoon's the man behind the trouble here in Gunn River County."

"Him?" Blayne snorted. "He's only a little man and——"

"That's right, Colt," interrupted Hardin. "Only a little man. But he was the big augur, the man who did everything from having Simmonds killed to arming the Apaches."

CHAPTER TWELVE

Rangoon's Reason

THE NIGHT was dark and still as Dusty Fog rode towards the deserted Flying Fish ranch house. The house itself looked deserted, except for a solitary light which showed from a window. Dusty did not expect to be challenged, or to find anyone but Rangoon. The small man would not leave a message just to murder him, that Dusty was sure of. There would be no ambush laid for him. So sure was he that he rode straight to the front of the house and left the horse at the porch hitching rail; stepped on to the porch and went through the front door. Along the passage he saw a door open and light showing through it.

Gun in hand Dusty walked along the passage and halted before stepping into plain sight. He stood still, the house was as silent as a grave. All Rangoon's crew had been in town and he had paid off his cook on his return, sending the man to Escopeta out of the way.

"Come in, Captain Fog," said Rangoon from the room. "I'm not holding a gun, although I tell you that there is one, fully loaded, on the desk in front of me."

Dusty holstered his gun and stepped into the room. Rangoon was seated at a desk in the centre of the room; the desk top was clear except for a Merwin and Hulbert Pocket revolver. Rangoon leaned back in his chair, hands on the desk top but not near the butt of the gun. He looked like a mild cherub but Dusty knew he was the hardest man he had ever met.

Slowly Dusty looked around the room. It was sparsely furnished and looked much like the living quarters of a soldier in a frontier post. There was a shelf of books like the one in Rangoon's office at the bank. The only reading matter was of a military nature, books on tactics, official publications, histories of the War. Dusty turned his attention to the two pictures on the wall. One was of three men, big men if the comparison of them and their muzzleloading rifles was anything to go by. They wore the pre-Civil War army uniforms and one was bigger in every way than the other two. This biggest man looked familiar to Dusty, as familiar as a half forgotten picture in a book. The man was also on the other photograph; it appeared to have been taken on his wedding day, his bride was a big, buxom woman.

Rangoon remained seated, making no move, his mild face showing no expression beyond the usual bland friendliness. "Do you like the picture of my father, Captain Fog?"

"Your father?"

"Colonel Grice Baldwin was my father."

"Grice Baldwin?"

"Yes, you've heard of him?"

"Why sure," agreed Dusty, remembering the photograph from a book he had seen. "I've read about him and heard the old Army men talk about him. Wasn't he the one who wouldn't take any men into his regiment who stood under six foot? The man who boasted any man in his regiment could lick two men—and he could whip any man in the regiment?"

There was a bitter note in Rangoon's voice. "That's right. That was the boast of Grice Baldwin, my father."

Neither man spoke for a time. Dusty did not know why Rangoon had left word where he could be found and waited to learn. At last he broke the silence. "We got all of your men. I reckon they might talk."

Rangoon did not reply to this. His eyes went to the pictures on the wall. "Did your father ever look down on you because of your size, Captain?"

"Can't say he ever did. Reckon he knew it wasn't my fault I didn't grow any taller."

"Then you were lucky. Grice Baldwin lived only for

bigness. He was a big man; the only one I've seen who was his equal is Mark Counter. Grice Baldwin lived only to have the biggest things about him. Horses, men, they all must be big for him. He married my mother because she was the biggest woman he could find. That way he expected a big son. The night I was born he took bets that I would weigh over ten pounds at birth—I weighed six, no more. When he found out I was not going to grow big, he parted from my mother. Sent her away from him, gave her enough money to live in comfort and educate me," Rangoon spoke softly but his voice held torment and anger. "He made two stipulations to his settlement. The first was that she never allowed me to use his name. The second was the most brutal, that she called me Horace. She did for he would have thrown her aside without a cent if she refused. She took her name of Rangoon again and told everyone she was a widow. Always the Army held a fascination for me, Captain, I've read almost every book on tactics that was written. My size and appearance were against me. I was too small for acceptance at West Point. I always looked mild, and fat. But I'm strong, Captain, far stronger than you'd think looking at me. Nobody would ever take me seriously. I would have been in my element in the Army but they would not accept me. When the War began I enlisted, hoping to be posted into a fighting unit. They allowed me in as a Quartermaster officer. Me, a man with more knowledge of tactics than half of the Army's officers. I only accepted in the hope that I would be able to get to a fighting regiment later on. But they kept me well back from the fighting line and I rose to major, tied somewhere safe at a desk."

Dusty sat on the edge of the desk, watching Rangoon's face. He could guess how the other man must feel. They were both small in a country of big men. Yet it was easier for Dusty. He had never felt his lack of inches, not when there were so many ways in which he could excel over the bigger men.

"You were the major with Hantley on the Cumberland?"

"Hantley!" Rangoon spat the word out. "I was sent to the Cumberland, near the fighting area, to check on some stores. There was supposedly no danger but I was given an escort commanded by a Lieutenant. Tom Hantley was his name, a dull, stupid and drunken lout with little or no command of his men. Through his stupidity we were lost and I brought us to the house on the Cumberland. We were attacked by a small battalion of Confederate infantry. Hantley wanted to surrender but I refused. He was scared and lost his head. There was a good cellar in the house and Hantley was never sober enough to fight. I commanded the men. I defended the house, Captain. Hantley was too drunk even to fire a rifle. Those rebs could shoot, Captain. They got man after man in my small command but we held them off. I used every military trick I could think of and we held them off. I was wounded on the first day, but I kept on my feet. One thought kept me going, that I would be given my chance at a fighting command as a result. I took a second wound on the day we were relieved and fell unconscious as I heard the bugles of Custer's regiment coming to help us. They found two men left alive. I was unconscious and Hantley managed to make himself sober enough to take the credit for the defence. There was not another man left alive who could tell the truth. When I recovered sufficiently to understand what was happening Hantley was a hero, a major, commissioned in the field as a reward for my defence."

"You could have told them," Dusty remarked, guessing what was to come.

"Who would believe me?" Rangoon asked pathetically. "Hantley was the sort of man who looked like a hero, I was not. I sounded a few people out, trying to say what happened. They treated me as the fortunate man who was with Hantley when he made his gallant defence. Inside a year nobody remembered I had anything to do with the fight, or any of the men who died to make it possible. Hantley was all they remembered. Look in any book of the War and see what I mean."

"I know. I've read a few."

"And never saw the name of the major who was with Hantley in any of them."

"No, I never did," agreed Dusty. "So you wanted to get back at Hantley."

"I did. The War was over when I was finally released from hospital and I was turned out of the Army. They kept Tom Hantley in on a permanent commission. I watched his career. It was one of blunder and missed opportunity, but that one defence blinded everyone to it. I followed him to the Black Hills, where I met Poggy. Only Hantley's coming down with

154

fever saved him there. He would have gone the way of Custer, massacred by his ego and blind stupidity. I waited, he was next in Washington where there was no chance of my getting at him. Then he came to New Mexico; to the fort near the Apache reservation; to his home town. I followed him but the very fates must have worked against me for he was sent to Arizona Territory and the Apache Kid killed him."

"Why carry on then?" Dusty asked, feeling sorry for the other man.

"I was willing to forget everything, when that infernal book of Hantley's came out. The people of town gave me a copy——"

"Which you threw at the wall from the look of it."

"I did. For once in my life I lost my temper. Those fools from Escopeta gave me the book to show me how a real soldier fought the War. One of them even said I should change my saloon's name to Hantley's Place. That was when I swore I would be revenged on them. I started to stir up trouble between the ranchers and the nesters, just in small ways, building them up for the Simmonds and Mahon business. I'd got Poggy out buying rifles and never stopped him."

There was a harder note in Dusty's voice as he interrupted. "So you aimed to arm the Apaches all the time?"

"Only as a last resort. I meant to arm them and give Tom Hantley some bad trouble. It took time to gather so many weapons without raising suspicion. I never thought I would need the arms; the business you and your friends spoiled would have been enough. It was a pity about Simmonds and Mahon, they were both good men. That was why they had to be killed. I suppose you know why?"

"Sure, kill the fighting men and the moderate-tempered folks wait for the law. Kill the moderate men and the fighters start fighting without thinking."

"Yes. You and I could have made a great team. It was to be war to the end and in war there are always casualties, the innocent suffer. There was suspicion and distrust, even after you showed them that someone was stirring up trouble between them. Nobody knew who they could trust, everybody was suspicious of his neighbour. Only I was never suspected. Even my men were not suspect, they worked for that nice, *little*, Mr. Rangoon. They never suspected me and I hated them for it. They looked down on me, those big men. Treated me as though I was a half-wit or something, all of them, none thinking I was the man behind their troubles. Only you suspected me. You—the Rio Hondo gun wizard, the Confederate hero, Dusty Fog. You recognised me for what I was. I meant to smash the others, even if I must use the Apaches to do it—One thing though, Captain, I did not think the Apaches would strike this way or so soon. I thought the county would be embroiled in a range war."

Dusty could see the tragedy of this man; clearly in comparison with his own life. Dusty was honest enough to admit he was well-known, almost famous. In the War he had been a fighting man, leading a company of Cavalry. He had done very well, but Rangoon could have handled a troop just as well given the chance. Dusty was known, respected and admired throughout the range country, even by taller men. Nobody ever regarded him as small. Rangoon might have been the same, respected and admired. It was a tragic waste of what could have been a very useful life.

"I'm sorry. More sorry than I can tell you," said Dusty, swinging down from the desk and facing Rangoon, hands hanging by his sides.

"Thank you. And now, Captain, what are we going to do?"

"I'm going to take you in, Major," Dusty answered. "I could have passed over your causing trouble between the folks. Might have overlooked your having Simmonds killed. I'd even forget about your having Lon shot down, we got enough of the bunch who did it to even things up — But I can't forget, or forgive, your arming the Apaches and endangering the lives of women."

Rangoon nodded, his face was still that mild mask. "I'm sorry about that. I've a carpet bag here in the desk, with money in it." He waved down Dusty's objection. "It's not a bribe, Captain. I'm still gentleman enough for that. It's the money taken from Simmonds. I'd like you to return it, or I will see Mary gets it. The rest of the bank's funds, less my own money are in the safe. I meant to try and make a fresh start away from here."

"I can't let you go."

Slowly Rangoon rose to his feet, eyes never leaving Dusty's face. His shoulders braced back. "I know!"

Rangoon's hand went down to sweep the Merwin and Hulbert gun up from the desk. At the same instant Dusty's

156

hands crossed, the bone-handled guns sliding out in that sight-defying flicker of speed which was the difference between a top gun and a man who was just fast. Rangoon's short-barrelled weapon spat as flame tore from Dusty's guns. The bullet ripped a hole in Dusty's hat brim. Through the whirling smoke the small Texan saw Rangoon reel back, hit in the chest. For a moment Rangoon stood; his gun slid from his limp hand, and he went down.

Stepping forward Dusty kicked the Merwin to one side and bent over Rangoon. The man looked up at him, pain and something else dimming his eyes. Rangoon laid a hand on his chest, looked dully at the blood, then gasped:

"Captain Fog. You've captured some of my troop?"

Dusty could guess what was happening. Rangoon's mind was going; he thought he was still in the Army, fighting against the Confederates. "I have, Major," he agreed.

"They acted under my orders, Captain. *Under my orders*—understand that—I gave—the orders—They merely followed—remember that—remem——!"

Rangoon's head fell back, blood gushed from his mouth, his small, fat frame jerked once, then went still. Dusty straightened up, there was nothing more he could do.

Slowly Dusty lifted his hand in a silent salute. "I'll remember, Major."

Wes Hardin and Mahon were the only men awake when Dusty returned to the farm. They came out to greet him; a few of the sleepers around the place stirred and rose. The cowhands and nesters were all staying at the Mahon place to help clean it up the following morning.

"We've got all Rangoon's men hawgtied behind the house, Dusty," Hardin said, looking at his cousin. "Haven't said much to them, but the last of the bunch who cut the Kid down are here. Want to see them?"

"Not until I've talked to Mark and Lon."

"See Rangoon?" asked Hardin as Dusty crossed to the house.

Dusty did not reply, but went inside and closed the door. Half an hour went by and Dusty came out with Mark behind him. A fire was going now and in the light of it Dusty looked at the men of Gunn River County. They were all present the leading citizens; Hollister, the ranchers, the nesters. Hardin watched his cousin's face and said:

"You want the Flying Fish men here, Dusty?"

"Nope, turned loose."

Hardin was a poker player who usually won more than he lost, but for once he lost his poker face. The surprise he showed was mirrored by every other man around the fire.

"Turned loose?" asked Hardin, it was all he could think to say.

"That's what I said. We got six of the eight who matched with the Kid. It's a fair swap for one wound. We got the man who shot Mr. Simmonds. The Apaches killed the man who brought them the rifles. There's been killing enough."

"What about Rangoon?" Blayne inquired.

"He's at the Flying Fish. I killed him. He gave me Mary Simmonds' money, the rest is in a safe at the bank," answered Dusty, then his eyes went to each face in turn. "He'll need burying. I want him burying in town, with a decent headstone."

"Like hell!" Hollister snapped. "Why should we?"

"Because Lon, Mark and I are all asking you. If you allow you owe us anything at all you'll do it—And when you put up the headstone don't put Rangoon. Put Major Grice Baldwin, Junior, U.S. Army. Retired."

THE END

158

THE COLT AND THE SABRE by J. T. EDSON

The Confederate Army needed arms. They knew where the arms were to be had, but payment in gold was necessary and gold was short in the South.

Belle Boyd, beautiful Confederate spy, knew how to get the gold but needed help if her plan was to succeed.

Fate threw her in with a certain captain in the Texas Light Cavalry – a young man who was already spoken of in the same breath as the legendary leaders of the South.

His name was Dusty Fog.

0 552 08017 9 – 45p

PLEASE NOTE THAT

The official J. T. Edson Appreciation Society and Fan Club will now be operating from a new address.

*FREE to members – signed photo of J. T. Edson.

*EXCITING competitions – autographed prizes to be won in every issue of the *Edson Newsletter*.

*YOUR CHANCE TO MEET J. T. EDSON
Send SAE for full details and membership form to:

> J. T. Edson Fan Club,
> P.O. Box No. 13,
> Melton Mowbray,
> Leicestershire.

A SELECTED LIST OF CORGI WESTERNS
FOR YOUR READING PLEASURE

J. T. EDSON

☐	08020 9	COMANCHE	J. T. Edson 45p
☐	07991 X	THE HOODED RIDERS No. 21	J. T. Edson 45p
☐	08011 X	THE BULL WHIP BREED No. 22	J. T. Edson 45p
☐	08017 9	THE COLT AND SABRE No. 26	J. T. Edson 45p
☐	08132 9	THE SMALL TEXAN No. 36	J. T. Edson 35p
☐	08241 4	THE FORTUNE HUNTERS No. 47	J. T. Edson 40p
☐	08279 1	SIDEWINDER No. 52	J. T. Edson 40p
☐	08706 8	SLIP GUN No. 65	J. T. Edson 40p
☐	08783 1	HELL IN THE PALO DURO No. 66	J. T. Edson 40p
☐	09650 4	YOUNG OLE DEVIL No. 76	J. T. Edson 40p
☐	09905 8	GET URREA No. 77	J. T. Edson 40p

LOUIS L'AMOUR

☐	09849 3	SACKETT'S LAND	Louis L'Amour 40p
☐	09354 8	LANDO	Louis L'Amour 40p
☐	09353 X	RADIGAN	Louis L'Amour 40p
☐	09352 1	THE BURNING HILLS	Louis L'Amour 40p
☐	09351 3	CONAGHER	Louis L'Amour 40p
☐	09350 5	THE LONELY MEN	Louis L'Amour 40p
☐	09343 2	DOWN THE LONG HILLS	Louis L'Amour 40p
☐	08157 4	FALLON	Louis L'Amour 40p
☐	07815 8	MATAGORDA	Louis L'Amour 40p

MORGAN KANE

☐	09425 0	DUEL IN TOMBSTONE No. 23	Louis Masterson 35p
☐	09467 6	TO THE DEATH, SENOR KANE! No. 24	Louis Masterson 35p
☐	09764 0	BLOODY EARTH No. 28	Louis Masterson 30p
☐	09794 2	NEW ORLEANS GAMBLE No. 29	Louis Masterson 30p
☐	09877 9	APACHE BREAKOUT No. 30	Louis Masterson 35p

SUDDEN

☐	08811 0	SUDDEN	Oliver Strange 50p
☐	09117 0	SUDDEN TAKES THE TRAIL	Oliver Strange 35p
☐	09118 9	THE LAW O' THE LARIAT	Oliver Strange 35p
☐	09063 8	SUDDEN – GOLDSEEKER	Oliver Strange 35p
☐	08907 9	SUDDEN – TROUBLESHOOTER	Frederick H. Christian 35p
☐	08813 7	SUDDEN AT BAY	Frederick H. Christian 30p

All these books are available at your bookshop or newsagent; or can be ordered direct from the publishers. Just tick the titles you want and fill in the form below.